Praise for bestselling author Leslie Kelly...

"*One Wild Wedding Night* features sexy and fun stories with likable characters, only to end with a sexy story that floors me with how well it resonates with me. Oh, this one is definitely wild, but even better, it also aims for the heart."
—*Mrs. Giggles*

"*Don't Open Till Christmas* by Leslie Kelly is a present in itself where the humor and the sizzling sex never stop. Top Pick!"
—*Romantic Times BOOKreviews*

"Leslie Kelly has penned a story chock-full of humor sure to bring a smile even across the Grinch's face and lots of steamy sex scenes so hot you will need to turn on the air conditioner to cool off."
—*The Romance Reader's Connection*

"*Naturally Naughty* introduces characters you'll love spending time with, explores soulmates you'll dream about and offers open honest sex and a hero to die for. Top Pick!"
—*Romantic Times BOOKreviews*

Blaze™

Dear Reader,

Some people like cowboys. Some like FBI agents. Some like princes.

I really like a smooth-talking bad boy. And if he has an accent, so much the better.

So when I wrote *One Wild Wedding Night* and introduced incredibly sexy bad boy Sean Murphy, I knew I was going to have to tell his story.

I wasn't sure I could pull it off. I mean, come on, a gigolo as a hero? But *Pretty Woman* is one of my favorite movies, so why couldn't a reverse of the gender roles work in a supersexy Harlequin Blaze novel? Fortunately, my amazing editor agreed (thanks, Brenda!). And the result is *Heated Rush*.

Personally, I think it turned out very well. The fantasy of being the woman to tame a bad boy has always been one of my favorites, and Annie Davis seemed like just the right woman for the job. Especially since at first she has no idea *who* he really is, or *what* he really does.

I hope you enjoy *Heated Rush*, which is actually the second book in my THE WRONG BED: AGAIN AND AGAIN miniseries, which began last month with my Harlequin Blaze title *Slow Hands*.

And here's to those bad boys...

Happy reading!

Leslie Kelly

LESLIE KELLY
Heated Rush

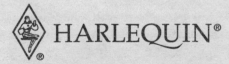

HARLEQUIN®

TORONTO • NEW YORK • LONDON
AMSTERDAM • PARIS • SYDNEY • HAMBURG
STOCKHOLM • ATHENS • TOKYO • MILAN • MADRID
PRAGUE • WARSAW • BUDAPEST • AUCKLAND

ISBN-13: 978-0-373-79412-6
ISBN-10:   0-373-79412-6

HEATED RUSH

This edition published by arrangement with Harlequin Books S.A.

® and TM are trademarks of the publisher. Trademarks indicated with ® are registered in the United States Patent and Trademark Office, the Canadian Trade Marks Office and in other countries.

www.eHarlequin.com

Printed in U.S.A.

ABOUT THE AUTHOR

A two-time RWA RITA® Award nominee, nine-time *Romantic Times BOOKreviews* Award nominee and 2006 *Romantic Times BOOKreviews* Award winner, Leslie Kelly has become known for her delightful characters, sparkling dialogue and outrageous humor. Since the publication of her first book in 1999, Leslie has gone on to pen more than two dozen sassy, sexy romances for Harlequin Temptation, Harlequin Blaze and HQN Books.

Keep up with Leslie's releases by visiting her Web site, www.lesliekelly.com, or her blog site www.plotmonkeys.com.

Books by Leslie Kelly

HARLEQUIN BLAZE

The Santori Stories

HARLEQUIN TEMPTATION

To Caitlin.
One of the greatest accomplishments of
my life is having given the world a soul as kind
and beautiful as yours.

1

GIVEN THE CHOICE between sticking flaming skewers up her nose and attending her own parents' thirty-fifth anniversary party without a date, Annie Davis would, without hesitation, reach for the lighter fluid and a match. Instead, she was reaching for her checkbook. Wondering just how far she could go—how much she could spend—to ensure she avoided a fate worse than burned nostrils.

"Twenty-five hundred, that's all I can swing," she murmured, reminding both herself, and her friend Tara, who sat beside her at an empty table near the back of the hotel ballroom. Twenty-five hundred was about as much as she could stretch it and still make her bills, as well as *eat* next month.

Tara, who occasionally helped out at Baby Daze, Annie's successful day care center, had come only to this charity bachelor auction for moral support. Her aspiring actress's checkbook wouldn't allow room for a guy auctioned off in a Salvation Army parking lot, much less one at Chicago's glamorous Inter-Continental Hotel.

If she were honest, Annie's couldn't bear the strain, either, and her savings account was strictly for emergencies only. Sheer desperation had driven her here tonight. Desperation caused by the thought of a weekend back home—sans a guy—being pitied and clucked over by all the women in her family, teased by all the men, especially her brothers, and set up by everyone else in her small hometown. Not to mention answering the inevitable questions about why she was alone when her entire family knew she'd been dating a nice, handsome man for the past several weeks.

Looking into her parents faces and admitting that nice, handsome man she'd been seeing had been a married jerk? She'd sooner add raw meat to those flaming skewers and call herself shish kebab. Wiping out her checking account seemed a small price to pay to avoid the agony. *Maybe the savings, too.*

No. Not a chance. Not unless Johnny Depp and Josh Duhamel both appeared on that stage, offering a weekend of pure carnal exploitation to the high bidder.

"Nobody has gone for less than three thousand so far," Tara reminded her. The petite brunette, usually bubbly and sassy, sounded uncharacteristically pessimistic. "Not even the wimpy-looking blond dude who made a complete dork of himself doing that pretend striptease."

Annie cringed, wishing she had a bar of soap to wash away the mental image of the pale twenty-some-thing doing a white-men-can't-dance bump-and-grind that had women near the front pretending to swoon. Ick. Bringing someone like *that* home to meet her family? She'd probably do better picking up a homeless person who wanted to make a few bucks for a weekend holiday in small-town U.S.A.

Now there's an idea….

It would definitely be cheaper than this ritzy charity auction. "Maybe I should just check out the park benches near the El. There's bound to be some guy who will do it for a whole lot less than twenty-five hundred."

"You're desperate," Tara reminded her. "Not suicidal."

"Is that any riskier than what I'm doing now? These guys are all strangers, too."

The only difference was they were being paraded and hawked in front of a crowd of rich, half-past-tipsy-and-well-on-their-way-to-being-drunk women in a hotel ballroom. Yes, they were offering legitimate dates—romantic dinners, beach walks, afternoon cruises and picnics—to the highest bidder. But these men were still complete strangers to *her*.

Besides, she wasn't even certain she'd be able to talk any bachelor she won into going along with her visit-the-folks date rather than whatever he'd offered.

So why was she doing this again?

Tara seemed to read her mind. "Desperate times call for…"

"An escort service?"

Tara snorted. "Sure, show up at your folks' with a male hooker. That'll go over real well."

"He wouldn't necessarily be skeevy. He could be nice, normal, handsome."

"Stop channeling that movie *The Wedding Date*." Tara smacked Annie on the arm with her rolled-up auction brochure. "Professionals like that one don't really exist."

"But I need a Plan B," she mumbled, knowing time was running out. *Maybe some decent-looking young man coming out of the unemployment office?* As long as he had all his teeth and four limbs, how would her family know he wasn't the one she'd been dating?

Or even three limbs…he could be a noble accident survivor.

Noble was good. Very good. Which was why she'd

immediately scanned tonight's program looking for firefighter, rescue worker or policeman types. Her dad would totally be into that.

Her family didn't know what her ex-boyfriend, Blake, did for a living. They knew almost nothing about her relationship with him at all. Just that she'd been swept off her feet by someone tall, dark and handsome. They didn't know *specifically* what he looked like. So she could introduce practically anybody and say he was the wonderful guy she'd been telling her family about.

Well, anybody except the *real* wonderful guy, who'd turned out to be nothing more than a wonderful *liar.*

"Stop thinking about Blake the Snake."

"Are you a mind reader?"

"No, you're just incredibly easy to figure out, Miss wholesome, blond, always-smiling girl-next-door. Whenever you think about him, your face scrunches up, your lips disappear into your mouth and you look like you want to hit somebody." Shrugging and sipping from her beer, Tara added, "Of course, you look that way when you fight with one of the über-mamas, too, but none of *them* are here."

Über-mamas. That was the name she and Tara had come up with to describe some of Annie's more difficult clients. There weren't many, but a few ultraorganized, ambitious, arrogant mothers of the children cared for at Baby Daze seemed to view day care providers as overpaid dog walkers. As if there was no more to watching a toddler than changing his diaper.

"You weren't in love with him, you've admitted that much. And you hadn't even slept with him."

"Thank God." Something had held her back, some intuition. She'd blessed that intuition when she'd found out her Divorced Mr. Wonderful was, despite his claims to the contrary, Married Mr. Cheating Pig.

"So forget him."

"I have. Almost. I just have to get through this weekend and then I can pretend I never knew the man."

"Tell me again why you can't just tell your family what happened? It's not like any of it was your fault."

"You met my folks when they came to visit me last spring. Do you *really* need to ask that question?"

Tara pursed her lips and slowly shook her head. She'd had a firsthand glimpse at Annie's life as the only daughter in an overprotective, small-town family who wanted her back home, married, and pushing out babies—now, if not six months ago. If they found out their "little girl" had had a bad affair with a married man, they'd harass her endlessly to give up her dreams of big-city success and come home where she could meet a *decent* local boy and settle down.

"Forget I asked."

"I'll get someone to play boyfriend, let them all see I'm blissfully happy and fine, then gradually stage a breakup over a series of weekly phone calls."

Satisfied with at least that much of the plan, she reached for her drink, still musing over a possible Plan B. The man she showed up with didn't have to be *really* handsome just because she'd told her family he was. Somebody much more plain and normal-looking than any of these sexy bachelors being auctioned off to support a kid's Christmas charity would do.

Beauty was, as she knew, in the eye of the beholder, and her family understood that. Just last year her brother, Jed, had convinced them all he'd met a future Miss America. His fiancée, however—a sweetheart whom the family adored—more resembled a Miss Pillsbury Dough Girl.

So maybe they'd think she'd simply exaggerated about how handsome her new guy was. Or that she was wildly in love, just as her brother had been. She didn't *have* to bring home a guy who looked like…like…

Oh, my God, like him.

Once again, as it had been doing all night, her gaze drifted toward the table, and the auction program lying open upon it. About two minutes had elapsed since her previous covetous glance, which was the longest she'd gone all evening without at least a peek at Bachelor Number Twenty, described as a good-natured rescue worker. An all-out hero. *Absolutely perfect.*

In addition, the man was an all-out hunk-a-holic.

As she stared at those midnight blue eyes, Annie's heart again played a quick game of hopscotch in her chest. Just as it had the moment she'd spotted him, this complete stranger, whose name she didn't know but whose face and body were as familiar as her last erotic dream.

Those cheekbones were high and prominent, the nose strong, the jaw carved from granite. Visible on one earlobe was a tiny stud of gold. His lips were slightly pursed in a sexy, come-hither smile that no *real* man could pull off and still look so damned masculine. The sleekness of his thick, nearly jet black hair—long, silky and tied back in a sexy ponytail—and the violet glint in those fathomless blue eyes simply *had* to be the product of a photographer with the latest Photoshop software.

Who cares? You're not going to win him. Not a chance. Not with what that last guy went for.

And suddenly, she couldn't stand to see who *did*

win him. Nor did she really want to see the man in the flesh, because, honestly, the picture had to have been majorly touched up. No man was really *that* good-looking in person.

Before she could move, however, Tara pointed at the stage, where the announcer was milking the audience, building things up to the final moment of the night. The big finish. Bachelor Number Twenty.

"This auction was your best chance, and this next guy is your *last* chance. So don't blow it."

"We should just go." Annie put her hands flat on the table to push her chair back. "This isn't going to work."

"Come on, what's money for if not to blow? We both know this last guy's the one you've had your eye on all night."

Had she really been that obvious? Maybe only to Tara, who had been the first friend she'd made when she'd moved to Chicago five years ago. Then again, her family had always told her that she should never play poker because she wore her emotions the way rich women wore their jewelry: blatantly.

"Have you noticed how much emptier the room is?" Tara leaned close, trying to convince her as much with her calm tone as with her words. "Half the women in the place got up and left after that last guy went, the international businessman."

Annie *had* noticed, though she didn't understand it. "Still can't quite figure out why though," she mumbled.

Ten minutes ago, when Bachelor Number Nineteen had gone for an unbelievable sum—twenty-five thousand dollars—the crowd had begun to rapidly disperse. As if some of the bejeweled, fur-wearing women had come only for that one man. Entire groups of women had flounced out, thinning the room considerably and emptying a dozen tables near the front.

The brown-eyed bachelor *had* been good-looking. But, in Annie's opinion, he couldn't hold a candle to the last man of the night. "I bet the high price scared everyone away because it means this next guy's going to go for fifty thousand."

"I don't think so." Tara leaned even closer. "The Junior League set is *gone.* Look who's left... Just rowdy blue-collar chicks like us."

Annie cast a quick look around, noting the laughter and easy, laid-back atmosphere in the room. And she began to wonder if Tara was right. These looked more like two-for-one happy hour girls instead of the Dom Perignon types who'd been involved in the bidding frenzy for Bachelor Number Nineteen.

Tara tapped the tip of a red-painted nail on the face of the sexy bachelor. "You can win him, Annie. And you *deserve* to."

Maybe....

"Look at his picture," Tara snapped. "Talk about saving the best for last. Go for it or I'll never speak to you again!"

On some days, that would probably be a blessing, but Annie was too caught up in the moment to think about it.

As the auctioneer began reading the last bachelor's bio, the remaining women quieted. Annie's pulse, which had accelerated throughout the evening as she pretended interest in some of the other men—even halfheartedly bidding on a few of them—picked up its pace. Her blood began a steady gallop through her veins, her quick, shallow breaths leaving her a little light-headed.

"You can go higher than twenty-five hundred. You know you can squeeze out a few more bucks," Tara whispered.

"You're pretty quick to empty my bank account," she muttered. *How much* do *I have in savings?*

"Raid the penny jar in the playroom. The kids won't miss one more alphabet puzzle. They hate those stupid educational toys, anyway."

"Shh!"

Willing the announcer to hurry up, she watched for a movement behind the black curtain, half wanting to flee to avoid disappointment, but wanting even more to catch a firsthand glimpse of *that* man in the flesh. Just to find out if he could possibly be real.

"I'll share my PB and J's every day next month if you end up on the verge of starvation." Grinning impishly, Tara added, "But hopefully you'll be so *satisfied* by your purchase that you won't be hungry at all."

Annie shook her head, denying that possibility to both of them. "This is a business arrangement. A weekend to get my family off my back, without them ever finding out about…"

"Blake the Snake."

Exactly.

"There's nothing personal about it. I've learned my lesson about hooking up with handsome, sweet-talking men. You're looking at a woman in complete control of her libido."

She meant it. Every word. She was confident, strong, secure, and certain she could handle just about anything.

But then the curtain opened and a black-haired god stepped out. Even from here, Annie could see the glint of something wicked and suggestive in his expression.

The photo hadn't conveyed the broadness of his shoulders, the leanness of that tall male body. He was wrapped in a black tux that looked as if it had been sewn around him, it fit so perfectly.

She told herself to be calm. Rational. To proceed cautiously. *A low initial bid, don't tip your hand.*

Then he flashed the audience a sexy, knowing smile, making those blue eyes glimmer under the spotlights. The sultry curve of his eminently kissable lips promised throaty whispers and complete seduction to every woman in the room. Especially Annie.

And suddenly her libido took control of her entire body and she sprang to her feet, an exuberant stranger's voice emerging from her vocal cords.

"Five thousand dollars!"

ONE BID. He'd been "purchased" after only a single shouted bid that had emerged from the mouth of a blonde standing at the back of the ballroom.

Sean Murphy hadn't been the most expensive man of the evening—the bloke before him, a rescue worker named Jake, he believed, had claimed that distinction. But he felt fairly certain nobody else had earned a five thousand dollar offer before the auctioneer had even opened the floor for bidding.

That had been the only silver lining of this ridiculous night. That and the fact that he'd at least not "sold" for less than a few of the wankers who had gone earlier in the evening.

"Thank you again, Mr. Murphy, for agreeing to help us out tonight. We've raised a very large sum of money. There are a lot of kids in shelters throughout Chicago who will have a much merrier Christmas this winter."

Sean nodded at the woman who ran the charity benefiting from tonight's event. She was a frazzled-looking, but pretty, dark-haired woman called Noelle something or other. She'd been trying to keep things professional, courteous and polite, mostly preventing the melee he'd envisioned, given the activities scheduled for this evening. "It was my pleasure."

Sold before a crowd of women. The realization that he'd gone through with it—and his name and photograph had probably been circulated because of it—was enough to make him sigh, knowing the response he was bound to get from his father. The old man always surfed the major newspaper Web sites, watching the financial markets from his home in Ireland. So if this showed up in the social pages, Sean was in for another round of "You're a disgrace, come home, bow down, be forgiven and do exactly what I want you to do," messages and e-mails.

"Who is it I have to thank for getting you to agree to participate?" Noelle asked.

Hmm. He wondered what the woman would say if she knew he'd been asked to participate by one of the rich, bored Chicago wives he occasionally visited when he was stateside. Now just a friend, she'd been his very first "client," who Sean had met six years ago in Singapore. Her husband had hired Sean to escort her around and keep her safe and…*occupied.*

He hadn't quite understood what that meant until the woman had seduced him.

In the end, they'd all been very happy with the arrangement. The businessman got his wife off his back so he could spin his financial webs. The wife got the sexual services of a rather inexperienced—but *very* interested in learning—twenty-two-year-old who fell madly in love with her. Sean gained invaluable experience, both sexually *and* emotionally, given the gentle way she'd let him down at the end.

And he'd walked away with money. A lot of it.

"Mr. Murphy?" The busy auction worker was still waiting for his answer.

Would she, as many women did, immediately understand—or *think* she did? Would she sneer at him? Proposition him? Grope him? Or freeze him out? He'd dealt with all of the above.

In the years he'd spent traveling out and about in the world, meeting people—meeting women—he'd met with all kinds of responses to his lifestyle. Not that many people really knew the truth about his lifestyle. Or about him. But he couldn't deny there was a certain prejudice, a preconception about what he did.

Sometimes he corrected it. Sometimes not.

In general, he didn't bother explaining. Least of all to a complete stranger. So he kept things simple. "I just heard about it from a friend and wanted to help if I could."

She smiled, readily accepting the explanation. "That's great. Some of our bachelors got their arms twisted by their sisters, coworkers, that sort of thing."

He sensed the fellow who'd sold before him, the rescue worker, had been one of them. He'd looked as uncomfortable in his tux as Sean would have in a pair of coveralls and a straw hat. Or, worse, in a classroom surrounded by squalling children.

Tuxedos? Well, those he could handle just fine. Given his family, he suspected he'd had one of them put on over his nappies before he'd learned to crawl.

"We're hosting a small reception down the hall for the winning bidders and their bachelors to meet and exchange information."

Uh-huh. Schedules. Phone numbers.

Birth control preferences.

Hell, maybe he was just jaded. There was no maybe about it, he was *definitely* jaded. Still, he supposed some of the women who'd come here tonight really did expect nothing more than a nice evening out in exchange for their support of a worthy charity.

But not all of them. Not a chance.

"If you'll excuse me, I need to get back to work," the organizer said, her attention drawn to a confused-looking volunteer counting piles of cash into a lockbox. Before her, tapping her fingers impatiently, was the petite—but curvy—brunette who'd paid such an exorbitant sum for the bachelor who'd sold before him.

She was attractive. Very. And young, too. Which gave him hope for his own prospects. Not much, unfortunately, given the glimpses he'd caught of the audience from backstage, made up mainly of women who'd appeared much older…and much *harder*.

"Have a good evening," Noelle said as she stepped away.

Sean murmured his thanks and headed in the direction she'd indicated. Might as well get this over with. He wanted a *real* look at the woman he'd be spending an evening with this weekend, rather than merely the shadowy glimpse he'd had of her blond head from up on that brightly lit stage.

Figuring out what kind of evening she expected him to provide shouldn't be too difficult. If he had to guess, he'd say it would take no more than thirty seconds to determine whether she'd known *who* she was bidding on, or not.

Given the way she'd called out such a large sum without any prodding from the auctioneer, he suspected he knew the answer. He got the feeling that was why nobody else had bid after her. Considering what had happened with the preceding bachelor, she'd simply scared off the competition, who had probably recognized the same note of determination in her voice that Sean had.

So the woman probably had heard some rumors about him. Who he really was, where he really came from and what he really did.

He doubted, however, that those rumors in any way resembled the truth. So he hoped that the woman hadn't given away a small fortune because she thought it would guarantee her a spot on his pillow tomorrow morning.

Nothing guaranteed that. Not unless Sean was well and truly aroused. It didn't matter who the woman was or what kind of balance she carried in her checking account. If he wasn't attracted to her, his services only went as far as being arm candy, tour guide, interpreter, or even, on occasion, bodyguard. Despite what *anybody* thought. The spoiled women. Their wealthy, older husbands who wanted them kept "occupied."

Or even Sean's own father.

Deliberately putting up his defenses, he entered the smaller room, where couples chatted quietly in shadowy corners and near the portable bar. A few of the women were laughing too brightly, a few of the guys were squirming under the attention. A quarter of the "winners" were probably two decades older than their dates but had had enough surgery to look merely one.

Only a handful of couples actually appeared to be having a normal conversation—i.e. one that didn't involve the rich auction winner trying to get her date, who'd offered a picnic in the park, to take her upstairs to one of the lush suites in the hotel instead.

He let his gaze travel the room, knowing he'd recognize the shade of *his* winner's hair, even if it had been lent a more golden glow under the overhead lights in the ballroom.

Then he saw her. One woman, standing alone.

She was blond. She was young. Truly young, not just faking it. And, as he approached her, he realized she was pretty. *Very* pretty, in a fresh-faced, wide-eyed, all-American girl way, right down to the freckles he suspected were dribbled across her pert nose beneath her makeup.

She wasn't drop-dead gorgeous, and didn't have that predatory look of a rich piranha, which meant she might actually have a personality.

This could work. Unless she opened her mouth and sounded like one of those brainless twits whose idea of fashion and taste came right from the tabloid princesses currently littering Hollywood.

But he doubted that would happen. Judging by her soft, silky yellow dress, the simple hairstyle—short, pulled back and held with a glittery headband at her nape—and her minimal jewelry, he suspected she was much more natural than that.

Then she spotted him. Those pink lips parted on a gasp, and her soft blue eyes—the shade of the cornflowers that grew wild back home in Wicklow—locked with his, and he knew he was right.

Because she was nervous. And absolutely not the predator he'd half expected to meet.

And he found her very—*very*—attractive.

Which suddenly had him suspecting this whole crazy auction scheme might not have been such a bad idea after all.

2

"GOOD EVENING," SEAN murmured as he reached the side of the woman who'd bought him for a night. "I'm sorry if I kept you waiting."

"You have an accent!"

He laughed softly. "Maybe you're the one with the accent."

"Oh, God, that was incredibly rude, wasn't it?" She stuck her hand out, which was so small, it practically disappeared inside his when he reached out and clasped it for a formal shake. "I'm Annie Davis. And you're…"

"Sean. Sean Murphy."

"Like Bond," she mumbled, "James Bond."

"Not exactly," he said, chuckling, "I didn't say 'Murphy. Sean Murphy. Besides, Bond was a Brit."

"You're not?"

"God, no."

As if realizing she'd insulted him, she nibbled her lip. "Sorry. I only like the older movies and you sound like Sean Connery."

So she had good taste, in Bonds at least, but obviously no ear for accents. "Connery's a Scot. It's not even the same island."

She appeared so flustered, he knew he shouldn't tease her, but he couldn't help himself. The woman, who he figured to be in her midtwenties, a few years younger than him, was too adorable. Especially when trying to come up with something to say without putting her foot in her mouth.

"What *are* you?"

"A man, so I've been told. An Irish one. Also your date."

She tugged her hand free of his, as if just realizing he still held it, and lifted it to her face, rubbing lightly at her temple. "I'm not very good at this."

"And I'm teasing you," he admitted with a soft laugh.

"I don't respond well to being teased," she warned him, frowning. "My oldest brother woke up with raw catfish in his mouth one morning because he'd started calling me Little Miss America after I got my first period."

Her face, pretty and creamy-skinned, flooded with color. Her hand flew up again to cover her lips as her own words repeated in her ears. "I didn't just say that, did I?"

Sean couldn't help bursting into a peal of laughter. "You did, yes."

"Get me out of here."

He stepped in her path to prevent her from heading for the door, liking her more and more by the minute. How could he have thought her merely pretty? When her blue eyes sparkled like that, the woman was breathtaking.

"I prefer swordfish. Just so we're clear. And while I enjoy sushi, I generally like my seafood grilled."

"Will you excuse me while I go hide under a table?"

"No, I won't, *céadsearc*," he murmured, taking her arm. Noting the softness of her skin, he caught the faintest scent of peaches and smiled a little. Not musk. Not cloying gardenia.

Peaches.

Unwilling to let her out of his sight, he steered her to a shadowy corner near the bar. He had the feeling she'd bolt if he didn't handle this right. Though why any woman would plunk down five thousand dollars to spend an evening with him, and then run away, he had no idea.

"What did you call me?"

A slip of the tongue. "I called you sweetheart," he admitted.

"That's sexist."

"You American women…you mustn't be so on guard. 'Twas only an endearment."

"How can I be your sweetheart when we just met?"

"Not *my* sweetheart," he admitted. "But I must say, judging by how many times I've wanted to smile since the moment you opened your mouth, I think you must be very sweet and very funny and very good-hearted." He grinned. "Stealth catfish attacks notwithstanding." Letting go of her arm—the silky skinned, soft arm— he added in a half whisper, "I'm looking forward to knowing you, Annie Davis."

He meant it. But the fact that he'd said it to her almost surprised him. Sean didn't usually let his guard down so quickly. Something about this young woman, however, had him dropping the smooth veneer and the jaded mannerisms that suited him so well in his daily life.

He wasn't flirting, or charming his way into her good graces. He was merely speaking honestly to her, something he wasn't often free to do with women. Usually he was paid to tell them exactly what they wanted to hear.

Except "no." They never liked hearing that. Sean, however, had no compunction about saying it.

"We *are* supposed to be getting to know each other, aren't we?" he asked. "So tell me about yourself."

He waited, wondering how she'd respond, this sweet-smelling blonde, who watched him with uncertain eyes.

"That word you said…what language was that?"

"Irish…some call it Gaelic."

She frowned. "Can you speak without the accent?"

"We still haven't established that I've got one," he murmured, for some reason enjoying teasing her, even if it might someday cost him a mouthful of raw fish. Cute, that.

She looked away a frown tugging at her pretty mouth. "Well, I don't think I ever said he *didn't* have an accent."

"Who?"

"You."

"Pardon?"

"I mean him."

"I ask again. Who?"

"It doesn't matter. I was talking about you…the you I *want* you to be, if you'll agree to it."

He sighed. "I think I need a drink. Want one?"

When she declined, he gestured toward the bartender. He pointed to a bottle of whiskey and motioned first for a finger full, then widened his fingers to make it a double.

The drink was in his hand a few moments later, brought by an attentive waitress in a short black skirt. She smiled coyly and brushed her hand against his for a moment longer than was technically necessary to pass him the napkin-nested glass. Then she sauntered away, a definite flounce in her step.

"Boy, talk about rude."

"What?"

"That waitress totally ignored me, not offering me a drink or even a glance. Like I wasn't even here." She rolled her eyes. "She might as well have ripped off her uniform and scrawled her phone number on those fake double-D's of hers."

"How did *you* know they were fake?"

"Oh, puh-lease…" Then, obviously having noted his inflection, asked him the same thing. "How did *you?*"

He responded the same way. "Oh, puh-lease."

A tiny twinkle appeared in those eyes and her lips quirked up a bit at the edges.

Liking that glint of humor, Sean cast a leisurely gaze over her, taking in every inch of the woman standing before him, beyond just the attractive face, understated hairstyle, simple jewelry and clothes. He noted the delicate swell of her breasts beneath the silk of her dress. There was no question of how perfect, how natural, her curves were.

He sipped his drink. Slowly.

Her shoulders appeared capable, yet somehow fragile, her bare arms strong, yet pale and slim. Her body was in perfect proportion, her height an ideal match for his. She could easily tilt her head back to meet his kiss.

And Sean suddenly found himself wanting that kiss. A lot.

"You obviously know something about women," she said, not sounding entirely pleased at the observation.

He knew enough to know she was one-hundred-percent female. And that she was instinctively messing with his head.

What, he wondered, would she do if he bent slightly

to brush his lips across hers, as he suddenly wanted to do? Would she pull away if he cupped her waist in his hands, rested the tips of his fingers on her hips and tugged her close? Would everyone else in the room see the brush of their bodies as an innocent hug, or as the carnal invitation he knew he would be extending?

"I should thank that waitress, you know. She helped me confirm just how stupid this is," she said, any hint of a smile disappearing.

Her tone chased away his sensual mood. He couldn't believe she had truly been jealous about the ridiculous cocktail waitress, whose overblown charms had nothing on the more understated ones of this woman. "She *was* rude to you, but it's cute that you're jealous."

The way she tilted her head to one side—puzzled—told him he'd misread her. Now he realized she hadn't been jealous. In fact, she looked almost…deflated. Morose. "That's not it. I mean this whole situation is stupid. I give up. Nobody's going to buy us as a couple."

Ignoring the obvious question—why anyone would *have* to—he asked the more interesting one. "Why not?"

Frowning, she gestured toward him—his face, his shoulders, his tux—then glanced down at herself. "We're not what I'd call a match made in heaven."

"We are a match made at an auction," he pointed out. "And that's all that matters."

"No, it's not," she murmured, those amazingly expressive eyes shifting away again, as if she had something she didn't yet want to tell him.

"What exactly is it you're worried about?"

"Somebody meeting us would take me for your secretary."

He snorted at the thought of him having a secretary. What? To keep track of his…appointments?

She ignored him. "Or your dental hygienist. Not your girlfriend."

Girlfriend? He didn't have those. Ever.

This auction was strictly for a one-date relationship, which was about Sean's max when it came to his personal life, anyway. Or, at least, it *had* been for the past several years, since he'd told his old man to shove his estate and his plans for Sean's future—including an appropriate marriage—and had hit the road, determined to find his mother and the other side of his history.

But he didn't argue, still wanting to get to whatever point she was trying to make. "Or they might take me for your mechanic. Who gives a damn what anybody else thinks?"

At that, a rumble of soft laughter escaped from her mouth, sounding so genuinely merry, he couldn't prevent himself from echoing it with a chuckle of his own.

"Yeah, right. Remington Steel showing up to fix my minivan. That's exactly what people will see."

A minivan…*horrendous*. "Who is Remington Steel?"

"He was a character on a TV show. My mom's favorite when I was a kid." Her brow scrunched in concentration. "Wait, Pierce Brosnan is Irish, right?"

"Oh, *that* show," he replied. "Yes, he is."

Sounding triumphant, she said, "And he's Bond, too! So I wasn't so far off."

He nodded to concede the point. "But Connery's still the best."

She rolled her eyes. "Well, duh." She looked away.

"My mother would be easy to win over," Annie whispered, as if working things out in her own head. "She wouldn't question the details once she saw your face and heard that voice."

"Are we getting closer to the subject now?"

She shook her head, realizing she'd been overheard. "No. Not really. It's still crazy and would never work, no way would anybody look at us and see what they expect to see, given the way I've been talking about you."

"Me?"

"*Him*," she said, her face flushing again. "Sorry." Then, under her breath, she added, "I can't believe I spent all that money. At least it's tax deductible." Nibbling her lip, she added, "I hope."

"I wish I had some idea what the bloody hell you're talkin' about."

"Come on," she snapped. "Not only would you *never* fit in my world, but anybody looking at us would realize we are absolutely nothing alike. We have no common interests, no emotional connection." She swallowed visibly. "Zero chemistry."

There she was wrong. Very wrong. He knew it, instinctively, just as he knew he'd be replaying their unusual conversation over in his mind long after they parted company this evening. And that he'd be remembering the echo of that joyous, uninhibited laugh tonight as he tried to fall asleep.

They had chemistry. So much chemistry he could feel it pulsing between their bodies, like brightly colored fireworks, flashing red and gold in bursts of heat and light. When he wasn't trying his damndest to decipher what the hell she was saying, he was forcing himself not to grab her and kiss the prattle right off her lips.

"Annie," he murmured, lifting a hand so he could touch a strand of that golden hair, "we most definitely *do* have chemistry. I suspect we could set off an explosion without ever going near a laboratory, you and I."

There hadn't been many such explosions in Sean's life. Physical gratification? Oh, to be sure, on occasion. But it had been years since he'd met a woman and wanted her on sight, for no other reason than the pleasure they would both gain from their physical connection. Especially one who had no idea who she was dealing with.

As Annie most assuredly did not. He knew that as well as he knew his own recent history. Which was *much* better than he knew his future.

I'll get around to figuring that out.

"You're still teasing…"

"No, I'm not. You feel it, too. Admit it."

The friction rolling off her body and reverberating back off his underscored his claim and gave her no chance to deny it. They were close enough to share the same inch of airspace, to feel the light rasp of cloth on cloth as their bodies brushed against each other, sending the tension, the awareness, into the stratosphere.

For the first time since he'd arrived here tonight, he began to wonder if he was going to be inside this building until the sun came up tomorrow. They were in a beautiful hotel. Upstairs were hundreds of rooms waiting to be filled with lovers hungry to spend the hot summer night in a heated, carnal embrace.

What would she say if he made such a suggestion? Would he scare her off, or finally pierce through that self-deprecating wall of chatter she'd been using to keep him at bay?

"I feel it," she finally admitted, dropping all pretenses. She said nothing else, just watched him, trying, as he was, to figure out what was happening here.

Something, that was for sure.

Annie's lips trembled and her pulse fluttered rapidly in her throat. Ravenous for a taste of her, for a sample of that smooth skin, he settled for a kiss—just a brief one—on her pink lips.

"Sweet Annie," he murmured before eliminating the inch between them and covering her lips with his. He didn't press for more, didn't demand entry into her soft mouth. Instead, he merely tasted her, shared a quick breath, inhaled the fragrance wafting off her hair—*peaches,* with the silky scent of her skin providing the cream. Then he forced himself to end it and back away a single step.

"Nice," she whispered.

"Very nice." His voice was just as low.

Much too nice to go too fast, despite how much he wanted to. While quick, hot affairs were nothing new to him, he knew from experience that if he made himself wait, the experience would be that much more pleasurable.

Besides, he didn't want to be one of those couples slipping out of the room, exchanging keys, heading for the elevators. He didn't want her to be one of them, either.

Regaining control, he cleared his throat. "That's enough for now. *When* we go out on our date, we'll talk a little more about this connection between us."

"Connection…"

"Don't make me prove it to you again."

She suddenly reached up, brushing the tips of her fingers across the tiny gold stud in his ear, twisting it carefully in a move that was entirely innocent yet incredibly personal just the same. He could read the fascination in her face.

"Would you, if I said please?" She still sounded dazed, her stare locked on his mouth as she licked her lips in such blatant invitation it drew a groan from his throat.

"Annie…"

"More," she demanded, swaying toward him in unspoken demand that he step forward to catch her body against his own or else watch her fall to the floor.

This time, the kiss wasn't as sweet. Wasn't as soft. And certainly wasn't innocent.

This time, when his mouth touched hers, she immediately licked against his lips, demanding a deeper intimacy. As their tongues came together in a quick, hard thrusting, her hands went around his shoulders, her fingers twining in his hair. Quickly forgetting the others in the shadowy room, he allowed himself to enjoy it—to savor the taste of her, the smells, the incredible softness of her body pressed against his.

Finally, though, a loud, shrill feminine laugh from a nearby corner intruded. Annie seemed to realize what she was doing—practically wrapping herself around him in a silent invitation to carnal pleasure—and tugged her hands, her mouth, her body away.

"Nice," he muttered, repeating her earlier description, which fit perfectly.

She nodded. "Very nice." Then she fell silent, staring up at him, as if wondering what to do, where to go, how to proceed from here.

Those hotel rooms beckoned again. And he sensed he could have her up in one with the merest invitation. It was so tempting.

No. This was the first time in ages he'd wanted a woman purely for his own desires, separate from his life, his job, his past, his family.

He wanted her for himself. Which meant he was willing to wait for her, to ignore the primal, heated demand of his body, which was unaccustomed to having to wait for anything these days. "Tell me where to pick you up Saturday night."

She blinked twice, her mouth falling open as she stared at him, still looking dazed, shocked into silence.

He sensed it was not a common occurrence. He pressed his advantage, not wanting to argue with her anymore about whether they would be seeing each other again. They would. Period.

"Don't even try to say we have no chemistry. Not after *that.*"

She hesitated, then slowly shook her head back and forth. "No, I…"

"No is not an option."

"God, you're bossy," she snapped, finally emerging from the sensual confusion she seemed to have been experiencing.

"No, I'm quite charming once you get to know me," he replied with a cocky grin. "Come on, give it up. What time shall I pick you up for our date?"

Annie crossed her arms in front of her chest. His gaze dropped, his eyes narrowing at the sight of the tender cleavage so temptingly displayed. God, did the woman have no idea how attractive she was?

Perhaps not. He'd thought her merely pretty at first sight. He now knew she was beautiful enough to have him rethinking his decision to let her leave here without him tonight. Especially given the uncomfortable fit of his perfectly tailored trousers. So he imagined she might not understand her own soft, quietly seductive appeal.

It was immense.

She tried one last time to resist, sounding anything but determined. "This can't work."

"Yes it can. We have an agreement. I gave my promise to the people running this show and you paid a lot of money to get what you want. We're *doing* this. If you don't like what I suggested for our date, feel free to choose something else. But we *will* be going out together."

With a disgruntled sigh, she finally gave up. "All right. You win."

As if there had ever been any doubt.

Annie stared into his face, her lips slightly pursed, eyeing him as if to see how far she could push.

Then she pushed.

"You can pick me up this Saturday morning at nine. Our date will last until Sunday night at six. Bring something casual, something dressy, and at least two spare pairs of shoes in case you…step in something."

It was Sean's turn to drop his jaw in shock. "Wha…"

She tilted her head back, challenge shining from those baby blues, dripping off her posture, and ringing clearly in her voice. "You said I could choose. And I have. We're going to my parents' farm for the weekend."

Her smile wicked, she concluded, "Hope you like big families… And cows."

"He'll never go through with it. He'll find a reason and bow out," Annie mumbled as she and Tara made their way out of the hotel, heading for the nearby parking garage and Annie's minivan—the spit-up and apple juice stained one that she used to transport kids to various field trips. The one somebody like Sean Murphy wouldn't be caught decapitated in, much less alive and a willing passenger.

Tara didn't seem to even hear her. "Are his eyes really that violet-blue shade from the picture? They're not, like, colored contacts, right?"

"Did you hear what I said?" Annie snapped. Her friend had been jabbering nonstop for five minutes, ever since Annie had strode out of the cocktail party, leaving a bemused-looking Sean Murphy behind her. Tara had been full of questions about the man's looks. Heaven help Annie if she let it slip that he'd actually kissed her. Twice.

Such a simple, normal thing, to kiss a man. And yet Sean's kisses had been a complicated mess of pleasure and confusion and yearning and surprise.

His mouth was as fabulous as the rest of him. Any woman with an ounce of estrogen would want a much deeper taste.

She doubted, however, that she was going to get it. Not after the way she'd responded, practically backing him into a corner to get what she wanted—his company at her parents' farm this weekend.

"Does he smell good? Guys like that usually smell good. Not like actors. *They* only smell like sweat, coffee and cigarettes."

Annie merely grunted. How could Tara continue to yank her chain—which she was, with these intentionally ridiculous questions—when Annie was so anxious?

She still couldn't believe the way it had gone down. She'd practically ordered a stranger to spend a weekend with a bunch of *other* strangers at a real farm a few hours outside of the city. Even more shocking, he *hadn't* laughed in her face or run in the opposite direction.

Sure, one of his brows had shot up somewhere in the vicinity of his black hairline, and he'd been speechless for a few moments. Then, with a twinkle in those beautiful blue eyes—yes, they were really that amazing violet-blue reflected in the picture—he'd simply murmured, "Very well," taken the business card she offered him and bid her goodnight.

As if it was all set. Easy breezy.

And completely freaking insane.

"He'll stand me up."

"Could you tell if that tux was designer-made? It sure looked like it from the back of the room."

"He's booking a trip to Siberia as we speak."

"He's tall, right? He looked tall."

"Rather than giving me the rest of this week to prepare myself to show up alone, he's going to leave me hanging—hoping—then stand me up on Saturday. I'll be brain-dead from stressing out about it and won't be able to invent a single excuse, like that my guy is on a top secret military mission to Hungary or something."

"Are we at war with Hungary?"

"I hate that you're laughing at me," Annie said, shooting Tara a glare, fully aware that her friend had been tormenting her intentionally.

Tara finally grinned and stopped harassing her. "For heaven's sake, will you stop it already? He said he'd be there. He'll be there. Why would he stand you up?"

"Oh, I dunno. Maybe because he looks like he's never heard the word *farm* in his life and doesn't have a clue that the filet mignon he enjoyed for dinner last night once wore a cowbell?"

Tara, the vegetarian—this month—threw a hand up in protest and made a retching sound.

"Sorry."

Reaching the garage, they got on the elevator to go up to the fourth level. As they ascended, Annie continued to imagine all the excuses Sean Murphy would make for not showing up. She couldn't think of a single reason he *would* show—despite how nice his kisses had been. And despite those sensual words and his even more sensual expression when he'd talked about their *chemistry*. She was almost swearing by the time they reached level two.

"I should have just seduced him. Got a night of good sex out of it, rather than expecting him to come meet the family."

"Heck, yes!"

Annie glared at her friend. "Do I look *that* easy?"

"No, you don't look it, but for a man like that, honey, the Pope's mama would be easy."

"I blew it," Annie murmured, not wanting to get into a how-sexy-he-is conversation with Tara, knowing it would surely lead to an oh-the-man-has-a-great-kiss conversation, which she *really* didn't want to have right now.

Those two kisses belonged to her and her alone.

Tara put a hand on her arm, lightly. "Stop, Annie. He doesn't look like the kind of guy who'd go back on his word."

"Neither did Blake."

If Tara's green eyes could have spewed flames at will, they would have been firing at the very mention of Annie's ex's name. "I have never even met this auction guy, but I'm insulted on his behalf that you'd even consider comparing him with that lying, cheating, womanizing slime bucket."

Sighing in remorse, Annie nodded. "You're right. Sean seemed like a decent guy." An incredibly handsome—almost magnetic—decent guy. And, judging from his bio, a heroic one, too. He was a paramedic. Saving people's lives—not trying to recklessly destroy them, as Blake had done to her.

Frankly, the man seemed like no one she'd ever known. "I shouldn't cast judgments. Maybe I'm just borrowing trouble."

"I'm sure you are. Now, tell me everything else about him." Tara wasn't teasing this time. She wanted the scoop.

"You saw him."

"From a distance. They wouldn't let us losers enter the cocktail party." Tara wrinkled her nose. "Junior League Nazis."

"Well, he *is* tall."

"Figured that much, honey. Give me something good."

"He's got a pierced ear and it's totally sexy." Even though she'd never imagined one would be.

Tara shrugged, unimpressed. Then again, she didn't read romance novels like Annie did, so she probably wouldn't get the instant gold-earring-long-black-hair pirate fantasy that had immediately gone through Annie's mind when she'd seen him up close.

"More."

"He has an amazing voice."

"Throaty? Like, talk-dirty-to-me voice?"

She shook her head as they exited the elevator and approached her minivan, parked halfway down the center aisle on this almost-deserted level. Annie tugged her small evening bag tighter against her side, sweeping a thorough, assessing stare around the shadowy recesses of the garage.

Despite what her family might think about her being unsafe in the "big bad city" after being raised in a nursery-rhyme town come to life, Annie knew how to handle herself. She clenched her keys in her hands, the longest, sharpest ones between her fingers, and suspected Tara's fingers were resting lightly on the small can of mace she always carried.

What a couple of Charlie's Angels. If a thug with a knife approached, they'd probably both toss him their purses and run like hell back toward the elevator. Frankly, that was the smart thing to do.

But for some sicko who wanted more than a purse? Well, the keys-as-spikes and mace were basic necessities when living in the city. Besides, she liked to at least think she was tough, if only to avoid letting her family's constant worries that she wasn't get her down.

They'd predicted robbery, rape, mugging…nearly everything except mutilation when she'd informed them she was heading for Chicago, fresh off the farm, after four years of commuting to a small, local college. In the five years since she'd arrived, she'd had her purse snatched, and her first apartment burglarized. Twice.

But otherwise, she'd managed to avoid getting herself murdered and proving them all right, which would have prompted the ultimate—if tearful—"I told you so" from her mother.

Her mother was going to like Sean Murphy. *If* he showed up.

Her father would like that he was a rescue worker. Albeit, the most elegant, well-dressed rescue worker any of them had ever seen. Again, *if* he showed up.

And her brothers would like that he was big and strong, and probably knew all about sports—even if it was Irish sports like rugby rather than football. *If he showed up.*

Her three annoying siblings would definitely consider him a step-up from one guy Annie had dated in high school. That had been back when she thought she wanted to marry the current-day version of Lord Byron, someone soft, soulful, vulnerable and emotional. *Blech.*

Although Sean Murphy was a gentleman—her instincts told her that—there wasn't one soft spot on that incredible body, nor an ounce of vulnerability in his cocky smile.

He was all mouthwatering, turn-your-insides-to-mush man.

"Earth to Annie?"

"Sorry," she mumbled as they reached her minivan.

"Tell me about his voice."

Remembering the question Tara had asked, she admitted, "He has an accent. The program didn't mention it—" which she found odd "—but he's foreign."

"Oooh, sexy. French?"

"Irish."

"Even better! Like James Bond."

Remembering her conversation with Sean, Annie had to chuckle. "Nope, Bond is English. Or Scottish. We never quite nailed that down. Sean's one of those black-haired, blue-eyed Irishmen who rolls his R's and sounds like he's taking a soft bite out of each one of his words as he utters it."

Tara's mouth fell open. "Good God, woman, did you spend twenty minutes with him or the entire night? You sound like he's been taking soft, sexy bites out of *you.*"

Feeling her heart thump in her chest at *that* visual,

Annie purposefully ignored her friend. And she managed to continue ignoring her as they got in the van and left the garage, heading toward Lincoln Park, where they both lived.

But once she'd dropped her friend off, watching to ensure she got up into her apartment safely, Annie could no longer ignore the voice in her head that had been echoing Tara's. She had felt like Sean Murphy had been taking sexy little bites out of her.

Removing bits of her self-control, morsels of her insecurity, and big, huge chunks of her resistance.

"I want him," she whispered as she entered her own quiet apartment.

Her four-year-old tabby, Wally, heard her and deigned to come to the door for a quick greeting, if only to see whether she had anything interesting to eat. Given her carryout lifestyle, she usually did.

Bending to pet him, she repeated, "I really want him."

And not just as a cover for this weekend's family get-together. She wanted him physically, as she hadn't wanted anyone in a long time. Including her creepazoid ex.

Given her recent track record, she had no business wanting anybody, or trusting her own faulty judgment. But that didn't change the way her thighs quivered and her panties tightened against her sex at the mere thought of Murphy nibbling her from top to bottom. Especially since she knew just how soft and warm his lips were. How delicious his tongue.

It was dangerous, unexpected, outrageous. But she couldn't help wondering if that chemistry he'd mentioned would be enough to spark something physical between them this weekend.

And whether she'd let it.

3

"OWNER AND MANAGER OF Baby Daze. Saints preserve us, she runs a nursery school."

Sean stared in disbelief at the small white business card in his hand. He hadn't read it carefully last night when Annie Davis, his pretty "winner" had slipped it to him after the auction. Now, though, since he'd decided he couldn't possibly wait until Saturday to see her again, and had dug it out searching for her phone number, he'd noticed what the woman did for a living.

Day care.

On Sean's personal list of things to be avoided at all costs, babies were two steps below jealous husbands and three above yappy dogs that piddled themselves the moment you bent to pet them.

"And she works with them. On *purpose.*"

All the more reason for him to call the woman and tell her she'd been out of line insisting he spend an entire weekend with her—on a farm, for God's sake—rather than just the dinner date he'd offered for the auction.

To be honest though, calling her to discuss the matter was only the excuse. Calling *her* was his main objective. He had thought of nothing else but the way she'd felt in his arms since they'd parted company last night.

But…babies?

He didn't *do* that.

Something inside him forgot that fact, however, as he pulled his phone out of his pocket and punched in Annie Davis's cell number. It was two o'clock in the afternoon. The little buggers usually took naps around this time.

He hoped.

When she answered on the third ring and he heard the crying in the background, he realized he'd guessed wrong.

"Yes?" she snapped, sounding out of breath. "Hello?"

He cleared his throat. "Sorry. I've caught you at a bad time."

"Sean?" she yelped, sounding shocked. "I mean, Mr. Murphy?"

"Sean'll do."

"It *is* you. Wow."

Screech, whimper, yowl… He heard all of the above in the background as he said, "I should call back."

"Probably. Yes. I mean, I don't usually even answer this phone during the day, but I happened to have it in my pocket and heard it ringing. No, honey."

Honey? "What?"

"Sorry. I'm holding a squirming bundle of male energy and he's trying to bite my ear."

He'd like to bite her ear. And he had a lot of male energy. Sean suddenly found himself envying that squirming child, though that didn't, of course, mean he'd ever want to hold one himself. His younger half sister was perfectly capable of filling their ancestral home with little Murphys. He felt quite sure their father would be able to pay off any future husband to allow the tykes to carry on the family name.

"I, uh, didn't expect to hear from you so soon."

"I figured we ought to talk about this weekend."

She sucked in an audible breath, and he could almost feel her panic through the phone. "You *are* backing out."

So pessimistic for such a sweet-faced young woman. "Of course I'm not backing out. I just want a little more information about what I'm up against. Other than cows."

"You won't be up against them. You won't have to set foot anywhere near them. I didn't mean that crack about the shoes. You won't have to go anywhere near the milking barns. And we don't have much other livestock except for a few horses. Do you like to ride? Oh, and there are some sheep, too, but they'll be down in the pasture."

Barn. Good God. And sheep? He'd seen enough of those creatures in the first twenty-one years of his life to last him until the end of time. Why had he agreed to do this again?

Her eyes, fool. Her eyes and her throat and her golden hair and her soft lips and her feminine body and her honesty and the incredible way she'd felt in his arms.

Well, all right then.

"Listen, things are kind of crazy here," she said, sounding as if she was about to drop the phone even as she mumbled something to the baby. "Can you call me back after six?"

"Why don't I pick you up after six so we can go have a drink somewhere."

There was more yowling, plus a bit of tiny purring like a kitten being petted. He didn't suspect that was coming from Annie, though he most definitely wouldn't mind doing a little stroking.

As he'd expected, he hadn't been able to get her out of his head all night long. He'd tried to capture the memory of her smell, thought about the taste of her, had replayed their conversation in his mind, envisioned her pretty face, the pert nose, the amazing eyes. Not to mention the feminine body beneath the butter yellow silk.

Oh, yes, he'd absolutely like to touch her until she purred. Whenever and wherever she liked.

Feeling that way about a woman he barely knew—being so vulnerable to her and wanting her so badly after such a brief acquaintance—*should* have been enough to make him avoid her. Reason told him to stay away from her until he *had* to fulfill his promise.

Instead, here he stood, phone in hand, waiting to see if she'd agree to see him again tonight. Almost holding his breath, unsure about her, as he'd *never* been about a woman.

Sean wasn't accustomed to being vulnerable to anyone. He never let himself get involved with anyone who didn't know the score and the rules of the game up front.

Those types of relationships he understood. Real ones hadn't been part of his vocabulary for a very long time.

A real one though, was the only type that could possibly happen with someone like Annie Davis. But that couldn't coexist with who he was, with what he did.

He wasn't usually a selfish enough bastard to take a chance, anyway, and damn the consequences. So why was he so willing to do it now? To risk hurting her—or himself—by getting personally involved with a normal, attractive woman who would never understand the choices he'd made in his life?

He didn't know. He just knew he was helpless to resist. He was so anxious to see her, he almost held his breath waiting for her to answer.

Finally, she spoke. "It's probably a good idea for us to get together and talk." She hesitated for a second before adding, "I did back you into a corner about this trip."

"True."

"Sorry." Then, sounding disgruntled, she admitted, "Well, no, I'm not really sorry. I needed you, you see."

Needed him. Not just *wanted*. Why the word should make Sean's pulse accelerate, he had no idea. But indeed it did.

Women were always wanting him. But needing? That was different. And at this point in his life, he welcomed anything different.

"I don't know what you're talking about," he replied, "but I have a feeling you'll paint me quite a picture tonight."

"Yes. I will. Let's meet somewhere, okay? Then I'll lay it all out for you and you can tell me whether or not you'll really go through with it."

Conceding the single-woman-safety-clause that required them to meet for their first date, instead of him picking her up, he murmured his agreement and waited while she named the place. Then he added, "You should know, Annie, I don't think there's much you could say that would make me give up the chance to spend a weekend with you. Cows and sheep notwithstanding."

He'd go through a lot for the chance to explore the attraction that had been so strong between them. Not to mention, finding out just how much she *needed* him.

"You might want to wait until you hear what you're in for before you say that."

"All right, then. Tonight, you can tell me what I'm in for and we'll go from there."

And with any luck, what he was *in for* included a few highly sensual moments with Annie.

ANNIE HAD NO intention of telling Sean Murphy the *whole* story. She'd tell him enough—in fact, most of it. She'd make it clear that she couldn't show up at the family party without a man on her arm, and she'd even try to explain why. Though, honestly, until he met her family, he probably wouldn't understand how serious the situation was.

She would not, however, go into details on the whole Blake-the-snake thing. Because that episode in her life was so humiliating, she couldn't bring herself to speak about it.

Thankfully, only Tara had any idea that Annie had been dating the father of one of the kids from the center. That was a blessing, because she'd been breaking her own rule against fraternizing with the clients.

Annie knew from experience that some young, pretty day care workers could easily get swept away by the handsome, wealthy dads who occasionally picked up the children. At the first child care center she'd worked at in Chicago, one of her coworkers had landed in the middle of a nasty divorce scandal that had nearly destroyed the reputation of the business. So the No Fraternization policy had been a top-ten rule when she'd buried herself in debt in order to open her own place three years ago.

And she'd broken it.

That she'd done it unwittingly was not a good enough excuse. She should have known better, should have seen through Blake's charm and his lies.

He'd just been so damned convincing and his life-style so convenient a backup to his story. His wife, who, Annie later learned, was an E.R. nurse with a demanding schedule, had never once visited the center. Not for an initial interview, not for a drop-off, a pick-up or even one of the children's programs. So it had been easy to believe Blake when he said his wife had divorced him and he was raising his precious two-year-old son alone.

Imagine Annie's surprise when one month ago—six weeks after Blake had started bringing the boy to Baby Daze—his *not*-so-ex-wife had confronted Annie in her own office, accusing her of sleeping with her husband. God, of all the moments in her life she'd like to forget, that was the worst. Thankfully, it had been late in the day. No other parents had been around and all her staff had gone home, except Tara.

Beyond that, the only saving grace was that she'd been able to truthfully deny having had sex with Blake. It was small comfort, considering they *had* been dating and had shared certain intimacies. But it was something.

"Enough," she whispered, the memories making her head ache. Forcing the awful images out of her head, she tried to focus on exactly what she'd say to Sean, who should be showing up at the bar any minute. She'd arrived at five-fifty, so anxious about the meeting that she'd actually taken off from work early, leaving her assistant manager in charge of shutting the center down.

It was very unlike her. But then, so was blowing an absolute fortune—including the bulk of her savings account—on one date with a stranger.

"Not just one date," she reminded herself. The price

she'd paid would prove well worth it if Sean could help her keep her family from learning the truth about Annie's rather sordid love life. As a bonus, it should also keep them off her back for another few months about her true single status.

"Talking to yourself?"

Wondering if she'd broken a hundred mirrors over the past seven years to inspire such bad luck, she glanced up to see Sean Murphy standing beside her table. God, could this meeting have started off any worse? He'd caught her muttering to herself as she nursed a glass of wine in a dark corner of a shadowy bar.

Plus, oh, joy, she'd just noticed that her bright blue Baby Daze uniform shirt had what appeared to be a spit-up stain on the sleeve and a smear of red finger paint on the hem. *Pathetic*.

"Hi."

"Hello." He looked amused, as if he'd read her thoughts.

He'd probably read her next one, too, as she studied him, top to bottom, wondering how on earth she was going to convince anyone she'd landed someone *this* good-looking. Guys like Sean didn't know places like Green Springs existed, and they most assuredly never hooked up with girls from them.

That fact was made more obvious by his appearance. Even without his evening wear, he still looked too hot for her, no matter what his resume said about his profession. Although, in terms of his clothes, he couldn't look much more different than he had last night.

Sean wore soft, faded jeans that clung to his lean hips and rode every lump and angle of his body. Some lumps were incredibly obvious, given her position, seated and looking almost directly at his middle.

Lord have *mercy,* could the man fill out a pair of jeans. She shifted slightly on the hard wooden bench, suddenly very aware of the pressure against her bottom and her thighs. And the very tender spot between them.

Taking in a slow, shaky breath, she forced herself to lift her eyes, noting the crisp white dress shirt. It was unbuttoned at the throat and folded up at the sleeves to reveal thickly flexing forearms. They were roped with muscle, lightly covered with dark, wiry hair, hinting at strength and power that hadn't been as obvious beneath the tuxedo. She imagined he'd have to be powerfully built, if he spent most of his time responding to accident scenes, saving people's lives.

Tonight he seemed the antithesis of the tux-wearing so-phisticate she'd met at the auction, but the attitude, the half smile, the gleam in his eyes revealed the innately sexy, confident man inside. No matter what he was wearing.

She grabbed her wineglass and sipped deeply as he sat down across from her.

"I hope I didn't keep you waiting, I don't often get 'round to this area when I'm in Chicago."

Her brow went up. "You don't live here?"

"Not usually."

Interesting answer.

"Where do you live? *Usually.*"

He waved a noncommittal hand in the air, evading a question that most people would consider extremely simple. The reaction was confirmed by his words. "That's complicated."

"For escaped cons on the run, maybe. Not normal people."

"I'm not exactly normal people."

Undoubtedly.

"But my mailing address doesn't really matter, does it? All that matters is that I'll be around this weekend."

"Just this weekend…" she murmured, before she could think better of it.

Sean nodded once. Though his voice remained friendly, his smile diminished the tiniest bit. "Yes, Annie. One weekend. I'll be leaving Chicago on Monday."

Annie heard what he was saying, and what he wasn't. She had to give the man credit—at least he wasn't making empty promises. He was laying it out on the table, what he could offer her, what she might expect from him. His terms.

He didn't say "Take it or leave it." He didn't have to.

She'd take it. How *much* of it, she wasn't sure yet. But, at least, she knew the rules going in and could decide whether or not that weekend would end at her front door when they returned from her family's place, on Sunday afternoon.

Or in her bed, much later that night.

"I understand," she finally replied, forcing herself to sound casual, completely unaffected by the unspoken agreement they'd just made. "Through this weekend."

"Okay," he said, though, surprisingly, he didn't sound entirely comfortable about her ready agreement. "Now we have to decide how we're going to spend it."

They were going to spend it perpetrating a fraud. But that seemed a little too honest to start out the conversation.

"Where do *you* live?" he asked.

"That's not complicated. I have an apartment in Lincoln Park. Not far from my day care center."

"And you live alone? No roommates?"

She knew he was trying to get more information, possibly even open the door to discuss her romantic past. But no way was she going there. "Just me and Wally."

His jaw stiffened. "Who's Wally?"

"My cat," she explained with a soft laugh. Remembering something she hadn't cleared with him, Annie added, "He'll be coming with us on Saturday. I hope that's all right."

"I'm allergic."

Oh, no.

"Kidding," he said, holding a hand up, palm out, as he saw her panic. "Lord, girl, but you're easy to get a rise out of."

"I warned you about that catfish," she said, unable to keep herself from laughing. He was…charming, that was all. Even when he was trying to get her back up, he was entirely charming. Easy to talk to, amusing, flirtatious but also courteous, his teasing sounding even more lighthearted with his lyrical accent.

She'd never met another man like him. And she *wanted* him with a kind of desperation that she'd never experienced before. The lust bubbling up inside her almost made her shake with its intensity.

Lust. She, little Annie Davis, whose brothers had put out a bounty on any guy who dared even *think* about relieving her of her virginity in high school, was *seriously* in lust.

The things she wanted to do with this man probably hadn't even entered the heated imaginations of the guys she'd gone to school with.

"Maybe I should meet Wally before we're stuck in a car together for a few hours on Saturday." The mischief in his smile negated the seriousness of his suggestion.

"Perhaps you ought to invite me to come home with you."

Oh, yeah, that'd be a great idea. Once she got him inside and shut the door, she'd immediately try to come up with some excuse to tear her clothes off—like, maybe because she got splashed with acid or something. And then she'd find a reason to leap naked into his arms.

That would be easy…she could just tell him the truth. She was so damned attracted to him, she couldn't help herself.

Too soon. Annie never acted on instant attraction. That had saved her ass with Blake. So she wasn't about to question her own judgment now by leaping into this man's bed within twenty-four hours of meeting him.

This Sunday, though? Within six days? Well, she'd give it some serious thought.

Not even bothering to answer his question about coming home with her, she asked, "Want a drink?"

He nodded, letting her change the subject. Signaling the waitress, he ordered a pint, which sounded perfect coming out of his Irish mouth.

His very kissable Irish mouth.

Just the thought of the kisses they'd shared last night was enough to make her want to sink low in her seat and relive it in her mind. Then fantasize about the next one.

"You're starin', Annie," he said, his voice silky smooth.

Shaking her head quickly, Annie mumbled, "Sorry."

"Has anyone ever told you that you wear your every thought on your face?" He definitely seemed capable of reading her mind. "You've not got a deceptive bone in that beautiful body."

Ignoring the flash of pleasure shooting through her

so-not-beautiful body, she went for bravado, knowing she was about as good at bluffing as Wally would ever be at roller-skating. "I don't know what you mean."

He grinned, but didn't call her on the lie, since his drink was just being delivered. Drawing a deep sip, he winced as he lowered the glass to the table.

"Not good?"

"It loses its flavor with every mile it's shipped away from Dublin, and the bartender drew it far too quickly."

"So you are *from* Ireland. Not just of Irish descent."

"I was born in San Francisco, actually. My mother's American. But after their divorce, when I was just a tot, my father took me back to Ireland." Though his tone remained easy, his body had stiffened. She understood why when he added, "And that's as much as we're going to talk about that."

"Sorry," she said, realizing the subject was a touchy one.

Maybe Sean had family issues, too. She couldn't be the only person to come from a big, obnoxious, pushy clan. Even if it sometimes felt that way, given the re-actions of many of her friends here in Chicago. They generally listened with fond amusement to the stories of her childhood, then treated her like she was the only refugee from the planet of 1950s Small-Town Hell.

Annie reached for the small bowl of nuts the waitress had deposited on their table, carefully picking one up and lifting it to her mouth. "I guess you'd like to know about the weekend now."

"I would."

"Then you can decide if you want to back out."

"I will *not*. I told you last night I'd accompany you."

"But I thought we were meeting so I could convince you."

He reached across the table and stroked the back of her hand with his warm fingertips. "We're meeting because I couldn't stand to wait four more days to see you again."

Wow. Talk about words going straight from one person's mouth to another person's heart. Or stomach. Or anywhere else…. Annie's thighs clenched below the table, and she scooched her legs together, suddenly *very* aware of the tight seam of her pants.

Because the words—plus that touch, and the intimate look in his eye—had definitely landed *there*.

"Since we're here, however, you might as well fill me in." Smiling slightly, he averted his gaze and let go of her hand. "Though, I think I might be able to venture a guess."

"Oh, *really?*" Her tone held unspoken challenge.

He tilted his head, thinking about it. "It's your high-school reunion and you're the last unmarried prom princess?"

She rolled her eyes. "I wasn't the prom princess type."

More the dairy princess. But she didn't want to mention the cows again until it was absolutely necessary.

Sean tried again. "Your ex-boyfriend's getting married and you can't stand to show up alone?"

"Not even close," she said. "My only ex-boyfriend back in my old hometown can't get married legally, at least not in this state. Though he and his *partner* seem very happy anyway."

Sean barked a quick laugh.

"I went through a sweet-and-soulful stage during high school," she admitted. "Primarily in reaction to my big, obnoxious, dumb-jock football-playing brothers."

"Brothers? Older, younger?"

"Two older, one younger. All hardheads. No sisters."

He nodded, then said, "Football, you said? That's like a tame version of rugby, right?"

She grinned, looking forward to introducing this man to her brothers more by the minute. "Right."

He snorted in visible disdain, then speculated, "I think I've got the picture."

"What picture?"

"The Annie Davis picture. The desperate-enough-to-buy-a-date-for-the-weekend picture."

She couldn't deny that title.

He lifted his hands, ticking off the details on his fingers. "You're incredibly pretty but single at the moment. You've had few boyfriends in the past, come from a small town and have a number of bossy, blustery brothers."

The incredibly pretty part warmed her, though her first instinct was to deny it. She *was* pretty...but not incredibly. Just in a girl-next-door way.

Sean, however, wasn't waiting for her to agree. He simply kept going. "So you blew a lot of money you couldn't afford in order to have a man on your arm when you go home for a family reunion. That way your brothers won't tease you, your parents won't be disappointed in you, and the rest of the folks back home won't pity you, harass you for leaving, or boss you around the way they did before you moved away. Am I right?"

Annie's jaw dropped. It was a good thing she hadn't popped another nut into her mouth because it would have tumbled out onto the sticky wood tabletop. That had been *quite* a mouthful. Quite an *intuitive* mouthful. "How on earth..."

"It isn't that unique a story." His brow raised in rueful amusement, he added, "You might be surprised how often I've heard it."

He hadn't nailed it completely but was close enough to make her wonder if she was really so easy to read. Did he look at her and see *only* the small-town girl with the spit-up stain on her shirt trying to please her family? Would he ever again see her as the stranger in the lovely yellow silk dress she'd bought specifically for the auction?

Again accurately reading her thoughts, Sean leaned across the table, his forearms resting on its surface. "Don't."

"Don't what?"

"Don't bring up that nonsense about us not being taken for two people who could be involved." He swallowed visibly, the cords of muscle in his neck flexing before he said, his voice low, "Because if physical attraction—want—is all it takes to prove we're a couple, nobody in your hometown is going to have one doubt as to why I'm there." His gaze zeroed in on her mouth and his jaw suddenly clenched. "They'll see the way I look at you and they'll know exactly how much I want you."

Annie's lips parted and she breathed over them, needing more oxygen than she'd previously been inhaling. Because her heart was sending the blood roaring through her veins at four times its normal pace.

"And they'll see how much you want me, too. They'll figure we're already lovers and the desperation rolling off both of us is because we're being forced to act properly around your family. While secretly, they'll know we'll be tearing each other's clothes off the minute we are out of sight."

She gasped out loud that time. Her clothes needed to come off *now,* considering how uncomfortably tight they were, how sensitive her puckered nipples were against her bra and shirt.

"No one will question a thing, Annie. I guarantee it."

She'd begun to lean across the table, too, drawn closer by his words as if they beckoned with genuine magnetism. She couldn't voice a protest—couldn't manage a thought—when Sean lifted his hand and slid it into her hair. He cupped her head, tugging her even closer, until their faces met, their lips brushed.

Her eyes drifted closed as their mouths touched and opened. The warmth of his tongue against hers made her shiver and the slow lazy thrusts made her shake. Once again, she was kissing Sean in public, not giving a damn that he had his tongue in her mouth when they were surrounded by strangers.

What woman would give a damn when this man was making oral love to her, filling her senses and driving all thought and inhibition away?

Finally, after a kiss stretching over several long breaths, he let her go. He pulled back, just a few inches, and, without hesitation, returned to their conversation, as if he hadn't just rocked her world.

"Now, forget about trying to talk yourself out of it," he said, averting his eyes and lifting his beer.

Seeing the way the dark liquid sloshed a bit on the top, Annie realized he was not entirely under control. He was just better at hiding his reactions.

"You haven't got the we-don't-fit excuse," he added after he'd sipped. "And there's no need to feel foolish or embarrassed because you want to do something to make your life a little easier for a while by getting your family off your back…especially since they have no business being on it. So stop giving yourself a hard time."

"It would make it easier," she admitted, though her mind was still on their kiss and those sultry words.

She leaned toward him again, making up for some of the space he'd taken by leaning back. With her forearms an inch from his, she was close enough to feel the warmth of his skin, yet not so close that she couldn't keep her head focused on what she had to do, rather than on how badly she wanted to stroke that skin.

Well, *almost.*

But since he'd messed with her by saying those outrageously sexy things, then kissing her—and *stopping*—the man deserved at least a little payback. It wasn't much…but hopefully Sean felt her body's energy wafting toward his, mating and mingling over the table, though he didn't acknowledge it.

"So how close was I?"

She had no idea about him, but Annie had been pretty damn close. To diving on him from across the table.

He chuckled softly, self-confident and self-satisfied. The man was cocky. No doubt about it. "I meant, my description of the weekend?"

"You just about hit the nail on the head," she admitted. "But it's not a family reunion, it's a party for my parents' thirty-fifth wedding anniversary."

"Long time."

"They're very happy, and they're great parents. Just old-fashioned, and overprotective." Curious, she asked, "Yours?"

His humorless laugh told her she'd set foot out of bounds. But he did provide a vague answer, even though it only made her more curious about his background.

"They didn't make it thirty-five months, much less years."

When he fell silent, indicating he was finished talking about his family, Annie filled him in a bit more on hers. "Well, when I said overprotective, that might not have captured it. My folks have been predicting my violation, destruction or murder from the minute I moved here."

"Big, bad city, hmm?"

"You got it. They'd like to think I'm miserable and lonely so they can throw every available man in my direction, hoping that one of them will stick and I'll come home for good."

"I'll stick," he promised with a wicked smile.

Yeah, I bet you would.

That body energy did a little tap dance on the inch of tabletop between their forearms. But Annie somehow managed to continue long enough to quickly fill him in on the rest of the details for their upcoming weekend.

Except the Blake details. She'd sooner toss away another five thousand dollars than let this man know what a stupid, romantic fool she'd been. Especially since Blake had not once, in the several weeks they'd dated, made her feel an ounce of what she was feeling right now, simply because of a kiss and the sound of this man's sultry, lilting voice whispering fantasy and desire.

"I think we can pull it off," he said when she'd finished. "We'll be able to convince your family to stop throwing men at you…just as long as we *stick* close together."

Licking her lips, Annie gazed into his eyes, saw the heat there, and knew he'd phrased it that way intentionally.

Damn, the man knew what he was doing to her. Putting thoughts of sticky nights and sweaty bodies and wild, hot encounters under the stars into her head. Letting her wonder—maybe letting *both* of them wonder—if their "act" might not be more convincing if they truly got to know one another…physically…before their trip.

"Well, then," he said, not pushing the issue, proving, again, that he was a gentleman—or merely possessed of as much self-control as a damned saint, "it's all set. We'll drive up together Saturday. We'll have lunch and spend the afternoon at your parents' farm, then that evening we'll go into town for the party at the…what did you call it?"

"The Elks Lodge."

"Ahh. Right. Then we'll spend the night together, and return to Chicago the next afternoon."

Spend the night together. Oh, Lord. There went the heart rate again. Not to mention the puckered nipples and the flood of moisture in her panties.

If the man was going to seduce her, she wished to heaven he'd just get on with it so she could decide whether she was easy enough to say yes after knowing him for only one day.

The little go-getter in her brain, who'd pushed her out the door despite her family's protests, gave a big mental thumbs-up.

She sat up straighter, striving to keep her tone cool and noncommittal. "We'll be spending the night together only inasmuch as we'll be sleeping under the same roof. I'll be much closer to that roof than you, because I'll be in my old bedroom on the third floor under the rafters and you'll undoubtedly be stuck in the spare room on the main floor, as far away from me as my father can possibly put you to make sure no hanky-panky goes on."

He laughed, that sexy, genuinely amused chuckle that sounded so natural when accompanied by the broad, good-humored smile. "Hanky-panky. You mean sex?"

So much for euphemisms. "Right."

"Does that mean you *don't* want to have sex with me?"

Geez, what was the guy, a sadist? Bringing it right out in the open like that and throwing responsibility for what would happen next entirely in her lap?

Most guys would do one of two things—tell her he wanted her right now, so they could make this whole lovers façade look a whole lot more realistic, or else avoid that question like the plague, hoping to work her around to the idea over their weekend then suggest a quick game of hide-in-the-haystack.

She didn't give serious consideration to a third option—that, despite what he said, Sean wasn't *really* interested in her that way. She knew he was. If physical attraction was a tangible thing, then the two of them would be buried in it up to their elbows.

"Annie? Cat got your tongue?"

Sean was watching her, speculation rolling off him. Expectation, too. Serious expectation.

He was not playing games, merely telling it like it was—wanting her to do the same. Despite feeling put on the spot, she had to admit she liked that about him. A lot. Considering what a liar Blake had been, getting hit with the truth and nothing but the truth from this man was refreshing.

"I won't deny the attraction," she finally murmured, staring into his violet-blue eyes, amazed at how they shone almost purple in the low light of the bar.

He continued to watch her, saying nothing, merely running the tip of his finger around the rim of his glass. The man had elegant hands—strong but not the rugged, brown outdoorsman hands of the men she knew from home. The idea of him using them on her made her quiver in her seat.

It would be easy—so easy—to tell him she wanted to have sex with him. They could be out of here and back at her place within forty minutes and in her bed three minutes later. Annie had no doubt that the night would be an incredible one. Just watching the slow, deliberate strokes of his fingertip on the glass reiterated that.

Part of her said she should go for it, that she deserved it after the Blake nightmare. Why on earth shouldn't she grab a sexy fling while she could get it? But another part of her, the bigger part that couldn't get over the guilt and humiliation, would never allow her to do something so reckless. *Again*.

At least he's not married. The whole promise of the *bachelor* auction proved that. But otherwise, she knew almost nothing about him, not even where he really lived. And getting involved with someone she didn't know, going even further this time by having wild sex with a near-stranger, was simply out of the question.

Knowing he was still waiting for a real answer to his question, she decided to be as honest as she could. So, meeting his stare, she admitted, "Yes. I'd like to have sex with you." His hand stilled on the glass, but he said nothing, as if knowing she had more to say.

"But I'm not going to do it. I barely know you and I just don't do the sex-with-strangers thing."

Undeterred, he offered her a cocky grin. "So how long does it take until we're not strangers anymore? Second date? Third?"

Men. Typical. But part of her couldn't help but be flattered by his determination. Hiding her amusement, she pretended to think about it. "Hmm…third at least."

He nodded, then tapped his index finger in the air, as if doing mental calculations.

"Three's right after two," she said, her tone dry.

He didn't stop. "I know that, *céadsearc*. I'm just tryin' to figure out whether we can fit three dates in between now and this Saturday."

"It *is* only Tuesday," she said, not sure whether to laugh at his playfulness or give in to shivers of delight at his utter determination to *have* her.

"What about last night? Having a drink together counts."

She shook her head and smiled sweetly. "I didn't have a drink, remember? Miss Double-D didn't offer me one."

He frowned deeply. "Oh, yeah."

"Besides, I don't think a drink would have made the cut as a real date." She was enjoying this—setting him up—though he hadn't realized what she was getting at.

Then he got it. Looking concerned, he asked, "*This* one counts, right?"

"Well, I don't know… It's not exactly dinner."

Without a moment's hesitation, Sean spun around, caught their waitress's eye and said, "Be a love and bring us two of whatever's first on your dinner menu."

The woman frowned. "We don't have a dinner menu. Just appetizers and finger foods."

Her mouth twitching as she tried to contain a smile, Annie murmured, "Too bad."

"Bring one of each of those, then," Sean told the woman. Once she'd gone, he turned to meet Annie's eye. "It's dinnertime, and even if it's naught but a bit of cheese on a cracker, I'm counting anything you put in your mouth."

The way his stare zoned in on her lips, Annie suddenly thought of a number of things she'd like to put there. Starting with his tongue. And moving on down his body to the many varied and interesting parts she couldn't see beneath the table.

"All right," she admitted, amusement now tempered with a very thick layer of physical awareness. "This is number one."

Nodding in agreement, he lifted his drink in salute. "Brilliant. Two to go."

She lifted her wineglass as well, watching him over the rim of it. Wondering if he could take a little torment as good as he could give it, she murmured, "But I'm busy tomorrow night, and Friday I have to work late."

"Thursday then." He grew serious. "Let me take you out on the intimate dinner date I had offered at the auction."

"You don't have to do that," she insisted. "I know I put you on the spot about the weekend. I don't expect you to really take me out to some fancy restaurant, too."

"I want to." He reached across the table and covered her hand with his. "If for no other reason than the chance to see you in that pretty yellow dress again."

She stared at their hands on the wooden bar table, noting the coolness of his skin, the elegance of his fingers, the perfect manicure, the expensive-looking watch.

How he managed it on a paramedic's salary, she didn't know. He looked like some rich, foreign prince. Judging by some of the things he'd said about his family, she had to wonder if he came from money, and merely chose to do something none of them had ever expected. As *she* had.

Then she glanced down at her clothes—the uniform shirt, the spit-up stain, the finger paint—and sighed. How incredible might it be to actually throw off the identity she wore here in Chicago—the nice, nurturing, small-town girl who took care of rich people's kids—and become a worthy companion to this worldly, sensual man?

"Say yes," he insisted, realizing she was waffling. "Please, Annie. I agreed to this weekend. The least you can do is join me for dinner."

Dressing up and going out somewhere special with Sean sounded irresistible. Especially when he appealed to her in that low, intimate tone, with his sexy accent taking those sultry bites out of every one of her defenses.

"Come."

"All right," she finally murmured, wondering if she'd have time to go out shopping for yet another dress. "Thursday it is."

Before he could respond, their food began to arrive. Annie deliberately met Sean's eye as she lifted a quesadilla to her mouth. Licking her lips, she bit into it, and saw his huge grin in response. *Now* it was official.

But she wasn't ready to let him completely off the hook yet. "Sean?" she murmured after she'd finished it.

"Yes?"

"You do realize that if this is number one, and Thursday is number two…our third date is going to be back on the farm where we're surrounded by my entire family?"

The man's mouth opened and quickly snapped closed. His broad shoulders slumped the tiniest bit as he sat back in the booth, eyeing her across the expanse of the table. He mumbled something under his breath, reached for his beer, then obviously noted the sparkle in her eye. "Brat."

"Hey, don't shoot the messenger."

He didn't give up. "How late do you have to work Friday?"

Seeing right through him, she replied, "Late. I'll be at the center, surrounded by lots—and lots—of screaming babies."

This time there was no mistaking the words that came out of his mouth.

"Bloody hell."

4

"Father saw your picture on the Chicago paper's Web site. Do you pay off reporters to splash your face in the society pages, just to infuriate him?"

Sean's twenty-year-old sister hadn't even said hello when he'd answered her call Thursday afternoon. She'd simply gone straight to the point, amusement lacing her tone.

"Hello to you, too, Moira."

"A charity bachelor auction? I thought he was going to choke on his morning biscuits."

"He's all right, though?" Sean asked, grudgingly concerned. The old man was a pain in the arse, but he didn't actually wish him ill. He just wanted him to concede that simply because he had supplied the sperm to impregnate Sean's mother, and had then paid her off to stay out of Sean's life, that didn't mean he owned his son, mind, body and soul.

"He's fine. Ranting and raving about the house, wondering why you haven't given up this foolish playboy lifestyle and come home to 'take your rightful place' in the family."

"That's never going to happen," Sean said, running a frustrated hand through his hair. He sat on the edge of his bed, a huge, king-size monstrosity only to be found in America. It dominated the bedroom of the elegant hotel suite. "You'd think he'd have figured that out after all this time."

"Oh, I'm sure he has. He misses you *dreadfully.* He's just too proud to say so."

No doubt about that. Their father was old school, all the way, and refused to admit defeat. *Ever.*

Sean had always known that, growing up on the family estate in County Wicklow. Traditions ran as deep and thick as the stone walls of the Murphy family home. The air within it smelled of the building's two-hundred-year history and carried a weight of responsibility that had suffocated Sean from the moment he'd been old enough to understand the words "our family name."

But it wasn't until he'd turned twenty-one and learned *just* how demanding the old man could be that he'd realized he had to get away. Because on that birthday, his father had informed him that he'd arranged Sean's marriage. Sean's father and his oldest friend had hatched up a union between their children before said children had even taken their first steps, like some pair of feudal kings out of the Dark Ages.

It still boggled the mind.

"Do you think he's learned his lesson?" Moira asked, sounding almost tentative. "I mean, I turn twenty-one in the fall. And Maureen's younger brother James is still single."

Maureen was Sean's supposed fiancée who, he heard, had married a few years ago and was living quite happily in Galway.

"James was such a bully when we were kids. Dad *wouldn't…*"

"Hell, no, he wouldn't," Sean snapped. "He might not be able to admit that he was bullheaded and stubborn about me, but he's not foolish enough to push you out the door, too."

At least, Sean hoped.

"If he does…I can come to you, can't I?"

He had absolutely no place in his world for a twenty-one-year-old girl. Not even a real home—just a couple of apartments in different cities in the world, nothing resembling stability. Nor did he believe that would ever make Moira happy. While Sean might have been desperate to leave home, his younger sister was never happier than when riding her horses or socializing with her friends right there in Wicklow.

But he would never refuse her. "It won't come to that, but, yes, Moira. You'll always have a home with me if you need it."

She wouldn't need it. People learned from their mistakes, didn't they? Their father wouldn't risk losing Moira, too, not after he'd seen Sean kick off the ancient dust of their ancestral home three days after he'd turned twenty-one. Telling his father what he could do with the ugly antique ring Sean was supposed to give to his "fiancée," he'd stormed out.

In the ensuing seven years, his father had tried many different tactics to get him back under his patriarchal thumb. He'd used threats, bluffs, false health alerts. He'd even paid to have a damned engagement announcement put in the papers, hoping to embarrass Sean into returning.

Sean hadn't relented. He'd had a small trust fund that his father hadn't been able to interfere with. It hadn't been a fortune, but it had been enough, at least, to start a new life, and that's what he'd been determined to do. He'd wanted to see the world, explore, experience everything.

Find his mother.

Funny, that was the one thing his father had most feared…yet the one that had softened Sean's attitude toward his father more than anything. Once he met his mother in person, he'd understood the truth. Hearing from her own lips that she'd been incapable of thinking of anything except her own drug habit when he was a child, that she'd been a danger to everyone around her, he'd realized his father had done the right thing.

One day, he'd tell the old man that. *If* he ever saw him again. But the way things were going, that wouldn't happen soon.

"I could come now," Moira said. "I love your apartment."

"I'm almost never there, darlin'." He said it gently so he wouldn't hurt her feelings, even as his brain numbed at the very idea. "And you'd be miserable in the city."

She'd seen his place in London, though she had no idea he had one in Paris and another in New York. That would just bring up too many questions about how he could afford his lifestyle. Ones he wasn't ready to answer.

He was well off *now,* but he certainly hadn't been rich at first. Merely determined to be independent and never go home. And Moira knew it.

Living simply and being careful with his money, he hadn't needed his father's. So that bullying tactic had been easily evaded. The threats hadn't changed his mind, either, nor had the guilt, or any sense of familial duty. If he owed something to the moldering bones of six generations of Murphys lying in the family plot, they were welcome to come see him personally to call him on it. Until then, he owed nothing to anyone and there wasn't a thing his father could do to bring him back.

Except stage a health crisis.

Sean had been about to board a plane to return to Ireland a year after he'd left, having gotten word of his father's heart attack. Then his teenage sister had called and told him it was a sham, that if he showed up, he'd be walking into his own damned engagement party.

Manipulative old bastard.

That was the last straw, the thing that had finally pushed Sean over the edge. That his father would put him through hell thinking he was on death's door just to get his own way *proved* Sean's demands for independence had fallen on deaf ears. The incident had made him realize that if he wanted his own life, he was going to have to separate himself so far from his old one that there would be no chance of *ever* going back.

And that's exactly what he'd done. City by city. Job by job. Woman by woman.

Starting in Singapore.

Along the way, Sean had discovered a few *other* things he was good at, aside from entertaining wealthy females. And he'd outgrown his need to shock his father out of his life. If the old man cared to know the truth, he'd discover that businesses from any number of countries around the world hired Sean to interpret, to make deals, to negotiate, to see to it that local customs were followed. He was an international businessman, plain and simple.

Let the old man think Sean had whored his way into his first million. Sean knew it wasn't true. And he no longer gave a damn about trying to convince anybody.

"So how much did you sell for?" Moira asked.

"Five thousand."

She yelped. "Dollars?"

"Well, they don't use Euros in Chicago, little sister."

Her snort of laughter said her surprise hadn't come because of how high the figure had been, but rather how *low.* "You're losing your touch. She mustn't have known who she was bidding on, Mr. International Man of Mystery."

"Yes, that's me, James Bond," he said, a smile widening his lips as he thought of his first conversation with Annie.

"I was thinking more along the lines of Austin Powers." Her snicker held no malice, just little-sister heckling. And maybe a hint of curiosity.

Moira didn't know much about Sean's life, which was exactly the way he wanted it.

Fortunately, their father didn't seem to realize Sean wanted to protect Moira from the truth. That was one piece of blackmail that might have worked. Which was why he'd made Moira keep their frequent phone calls, friendly correspondence and occasional out-of-town meetings a secret from the man.

"How's your mother?" he asked, changing the subject.

"Rich, miserable and hitting the martinis by noon. Yours?"

"Poor, happy, clean and sober." *Finally.*

"Sounds about right. Money doesn't buy happiness."

Knowing his sister's love of all things designer, he laughed. "No, but you wouldn't last a day without your limitless gold card." And neither would Sean's stepmother. While his own mother, who'd once allowed herself to be bought out of her only child's existence because of her screwed-up choices and lifestyle, now wouldn't take a penny he offered and was perfectly happy living as a starving artist in San Francisco.

There was a lesson in that.

After chatting a few more minutes, Sean finished his conversation with his sister and hung up. Glancing at the clock, he sent up a mental thank-you to Moira for the call. At least she'd distracted him for a while.

But how was he going to fill the rest of the day, waiting to see Annie again? Yesterday had been hectic with business meetings—financial stuff only, not any kind of *social* business. Though he could probably have found plenty of women eager for his company on this trip, the only one he was interested in seeing was the sexy blonde who'd *bought* him for the weekend. The one he wasn't going to see for another few hours.

Sean leaned back on the plush bed, knowing how he could fill that time if she were here with him.

Glancing around, he found himself wishing he'd stayed at another hotel—the one he usually frequented when in Chicago, which was older and had a lot of character. Though impeccable and tastefully decorated, this room was cold and impersonal.

And it instantly made him think of hot, sweaty sex.

He'd come here on impulse, having visited previously just after New Year's. On that occasion, he'd been asked to come by a friend he'd met in Japan. That friend—Brandon—had wanted to give his girlfriend the kind of kinky fantasy women often whispered about but seldom actually went through with.

A night with two men.

Sean had agreed, with some preestablished rules about how far things could go. They'd gone pretty far, but not all the way. Which, he sensed, had been a great relief to Brandon.

"Better you than me, my friend," he muttered. Because while the night had been incredibly erotic—and pleasurable—there wasn't a chance in hell that Sean would ever share a woman he loved with another man. Not even to fulfill her own fantasies, selfish bastard that he was.

He didn't share. And the very idea of seeing another man put his hands on Annie made him want to do violence.

"Jaysus, man, you're losing it," he muttered. He sat up on the bed, dropping his legs over the side. "You barely know her."

Why on earth *her* name—and face—would come to mind, and would inspire such a reaction, he honestly didn't know. Nor was he sure that he liked it. That kind of reaction hinted at some kind of emotional connection between them, when all Sean had any interest in was the physical.

So back out, a small voice in his brain whispered.

It might be wise to retreat, now, before things got any more heated between them. He couldn't stand her up this weekend…he knew how important that was to her. But tonight?

He glanced at the clock. After four. If he was going through with his date with Annie, he probably ought to get a move on. And if he wasn't….

He honestly couldn't decide. But knowing he didn't have time to fool around, he headed for the shower, using the hot water and the steam to clear his head, let him think straight.

"Second date or not?" he muttered.

The question reminded him of their conversation at the bar the other night, the way she'd made him work for that second date. And, hopefully, a third. God, but she'd been adorable.

Thoughts of Annie's gentle laugh, her bright smile,

her slim, graceful body, had filled his head often since then. Now, though, what he remembered most was the smell of her. That soft, peaches and cream smell. He didn't know if it came from her shampoo, body lotion, or some kind of perfume. He only knew that whenever he thought about it, he wanted to taste her. To savor her like a ripe, juicy piece of fruit.

Right here in the luxurious bathroom would be a nice place to start doing all the things he wanted to do to her. He'd love to stand Annie in front of him in the shower, aiming the twin jets of water pulsing from the two showerheads directly at her.

Sean would tuck in behind her, his chest to her back, his cock nestled up against her soft, sweet ass, their bodies slick with soap. Though the tension of it would kill him—and he'd be dying to lean her forward and clench her hips so he could slide up into her from behind—he'd show restraint. Go slow.

He'd soap his hands, then reach around to delicately wash her. Thoroughly. Intimately. Giving careful attention to her throat, her neck, her beautiful breasts.

Sliding one leg between hers, he'd hold her thighs apart, exposing her sex to the stream of hot liquid cascading down from above. And then he'd help the water in its quest to pleasure her. He'd use his touch, the feel of his hot breath on her skin, his sultry whispers about how much he wanted her, to bring Annie's arousal level to a fever pitch.

"God, yes," he groaned, realizing he was already there.

His body had reacted to the heated thoughts and the stroke of his own hand as he washed himself.

Knowing there was no way in hell he'd give up the chance to see her tonight—to have their second date as they inched closer to that ever-important third one—

Sean gave himself over to it. To fantasy, to sensation, to anticipation.

His mind filled with images of Annie with her head thrown back as he pleasured her. Her pink-tipped breasts arching toward his mouth. It was *her* hand on his cock, wrapped tight, stroking him into madness. *Her* touch bringing him higher and higher.

His mind suddenly conjured up the scent of peaches.

Leaning one arm against the slick tile wall, he pumped into his own fist, practically feeling Annie's tight little body clenching him, wringing him dry of thought and sensation. Until finally his every muscle stiffened. A roar of heat rushed through his veins and he came with a soft groan of pleasure.

It was enough for now. But it couldn't begin to compare, he knew, to what was waiting for him when he did truly make love to Annie Davis.

Which meant the answer was yes to their second date.

ANNIE HADN'T HAD to go shopping for a dress. She wasn't a clotheshorse, and seldom had use for dressy outfits. But that didn't mean she hadn't done what every red-blooded American woman did whenever she passed an end-of-season clearance rack—grab a little black cocktail dress if she saw the right size.

She'd forgotten about the ones she'd stashed away at the back of her closet in recent years. Not just in black, but in red and navy, too. All with the tags still attached.

But she didn't decide to wear one of those. Because Annie had a problem. She did not know for *sure* that Sean was taking her somewhere that would require a cocktail dress.

According to what she'd just discovered, a pair of jeans and a baseball cap might be more appropriate.

"You are such a contradiction," she mumbled, staring at Sean's photo in the slick brochure from Monday night's auction.

She had grabbed the program from the center console of her minivan when she got home from work, shoving the usual contents—empty bottle, rattle, spare pacifier, blanket—out of the way. Hoping to find out the name of the restaurant where they'd be dining so she could decide what to wear, she'd read the paragraph beneath his picture. And had been thoroughly confused.

"A home game at Wrigley," she read again. "Followed by wings and beer at a pub."

That *so* didn't sound like the kind of dinner she'd envisioned. Sean had specifically mentioned her yellow dress, and even the most clueless of guys—which he wasn't—would know a woman wouldn't wear something like that to a baseball game.

Wally, who was sprawled in his favorite so-not-cat-like spread-eagle position on the couch, lifted his head to see if she was speaking to him. Not that he usually paid any attention, at least, not unless she had food. "Go back to sleep," she said. "Better yet, go into my room and stay there so you can't be mean to Sean."

He ignored her. Wally wasn't the most friendly creature. When her brother Jed had come to visit, the disdainful cat had actually peed on his shoes.

Picturing the horrendous possibilities, she picked Wally up and took him with her to the bedroom, bringing the brochure along, too. Now that she'd caught sight of that picture again, her eyes kept going back to it, acknowledging that, yes, she truly was going on a date with *that* incredible man.

Giving in to a sudden impulse, Annie tore Sean's page out of the program so she could save it. She was obviously channeling her Tiger-Beat-Magazine-loving tween self. Because if she drew hearts around his face and wrote "Sean Loves Annie" in spiky cursive handwriting, it would look much like the artwork that had adorned her bedroom walls when she'd been twelve.

"Crazy," she said, laughing at herself for the silliness. Tara would have such a field day with this one.

Realizing she was running out of time, Annie showered, put on the basics in terms of makeup, and left her hair down in its usual slick bob.

But that didn't solve the problem of the clothes. That was why, when she heard a knock on her apartment door at seven o'clock, she was wearing nothing but a bra and panties, covered with a short, silky blue robe.

When she answered and saw Sean standing there in a dark, tailored suit, she knew she should have gone with a dress.

"Good God, woman, are you tryin' to kill me here?"

He stared at her from the doorway, his eyes narrowing as he noted the deep vee of the robe and the tight cinch of the tie around her waist. She could almost see the hunger wash over him, like a wave of warm water, as he parted his lips and breathed audibly across them.

"Give me a piece of pizza," he muttered. "We'll call this number two and I'll come back in an hour for our third date."

Pizza wasn't a food anyone would associate with someone who looked like him. Not tonight, anyway.

His long, dark hair was pulled back into a short ponytail, his ruggedly handsome freshly shaved. The impeccably tailored jacket highlighted the broad shoulders, the splashy colors of his tie completely in style. The trousers skimmed over his lean hips and she'd wager his shoes were Italian.

And he was a rescue worker? Good grief, the man looked like he should be on the pages of a Hollywood magazine. She couldn't help thinking any ambulance he stepped out of at a rescue scene could only be on a movie set.

She really needed to ask him where he worked.

Wherever it was, pizza just wouldn't cut it. Caviar, maybe—though Annie had never tasted it, and had no desire to.

"Or have you changed your mind about that third date requirement?" he asked, sounding hopeful as he stepped inside.

Annie pushed the door closed, then looked up at him, wanting suddenly to lean up on tiptoe and nibble on that little gold stud in his ear. "This wasn't intentional. I wasn't sure what to wear," she replied.

Her voice was shaky, her attention still on that tiny nub of gold. She had absolutely no doubt that if she nibbled, he'd have her on her back in two minutes flat.

So take a bite.

"Please tell me you're not one of *those* women."

"Those women?"

"I mean, I'm not going to have to stand here for an hour while you try on everything in your closet and get my opinion?" His expression suddenly wolfish, he added, "Though, of course, if you want my opinion on what to wear *under* your dress, I'd be happy to oblige."

Hmm. Tempting. Especially since she was wearing a peach-colored bra and panty set that brought a warm glow to her skin.

Forget it. You're being careful now, remember? Three dates isn't too much to expect.

Yeah, yeah. The woman who'd been knocked down

by romance recently knew the little voice of caution was right.

The one who hadn't had a lover in a year—and was looking at the sexiest man she'd ever seen—was saying, "Screw it." Especially since she knew Sean would only be around through this weekend. Then he'd be leaving, gone back to…wherever. Exiting her life as quickly and decisively as he'd entered it.

The realization stung, hitting her hard somewhere deep inside, where she *shouldn't* already be affected by a near-stranger.

So do it. Take him while you've got the chance.

God, it was tempting. And if it hadn't been for her recent experience with Blake, she might well have done it. As it was, however, she just couldn't. "I think I can manage. I'll dress quickly and we can go."

He wasn't paying attention. Sean's gaze had moved down and his clenched jaw and stiffened shoulders told her he was definitely affected by what he saw.

She glanced down and realized why. Her mouth might have been saying they needed to go, but her hands obviously hadn't gotten the message. Because she'd released her grip on the edges of the robe. The silky fabric had slid apart, deepening the vee. It now extended all the way down to the loose tie at the waist, revealing her bra…and a whole lot of skin.

"Peach," he whispered. "My new favorite."

Sean stared at her with such raw want, such masculine intensity, she didn't know whether to be drawn forward, or intimidated into stepping back.

She simply wasn't used to it. Annie Davis, the glorified babysitter, just wasn't the type to inspire the kind of raw desire she saw in this man's eyes. And while it thrilled her, it also scared her half to death. Because all her protestations about being careful and going slow were on the verge of flying out the window.

"I have to taste you," he said.

And there they went.

Sean eliminated the space between them without another word. He walked right into her mouth, capturing her lips with his, his tongue plunging fast and deep.

Already shaking from the pleasure of it, Annie lifted her arms to encircle his neck, and tilted her head for more. More heat, more wild thrusts, more sensation.

His big, strong hands separated the robe, pushing it wide so he could stroke her waist. His fingers skimmed up her body, scraping across her midriff, then sliding around to capture her hips. He tugged her against him, until Annie could feel the big, hard ridge of his erection pressing against her.

Pure, undiluted need flooded her. Her panties tightened against her sex, and she arched harder against him, desperate for more. "Sean," she groaned against his mouth.

He kissed his way along her jaw and down, licking, tasting, even biting a little as he reached her neck. Every touch brought another quiver, each taste sending another thrill through her until her legs shook.

"I've been dreaming about peaches," he admitted as he kissed his way down her. Gently pushing her until the backs of her legs reached the edge of the sofa, he lowered her onto the arm of it. "Let me see how sweet you taste."

The very idea of refusing him was ridiculous. She wanted his mouth on about a hundred different spots on her body—followed by a hundred more.

"Please do," she whispered, shrugging her shoulders to let the robe fall off. She tossed it away, then lifted her hands to his hair, twining her fingers in its inky black strands.

Sean bent to nuzzle in the seam between her breasts, breathing heavily, as if he wanted to inhale her. Annie's skin puckered, her nipples hardening against the lace of her bra. Noticing, Sean rubbed his cheek against the tip of one, even as he ran his finger along the swell of the other.

She arched toward his touch, wanting more than the tauntingly light caress he was giving her. As if knowing it, Sean drew the tension out even more, toying with her, moving back and forth to breathe on her nipples through the fabric, until Annie was squirming.

She squirmed so much she fell back onto the couch.

"Don't leave without me," he said with a laugh as he followed her down, kneeling on the floor in front of her.

"I'm not going *anywhere* without you," she said, letting him hear the innuendo in her words.

"I don't know, love," he said as he moved his mouth back to her body, now tasting the vulnerable flesh below her breasts. "I'd like to see how far I can make you go."

Then he proceeded to find out. Sean lowered the strap of her bra, kissing his way down every inch of her breast as he revealed it. She was a living bundle of nerve endings, waiting for the touch she most craved, and when he gave it to her—covering her nipple with his mouth—she cried out.

He drew deep, sucked hard, until she felt the draw between her legs. Uncovering her other breast, he toyed with the taut peak, his fingers feeling almost as good as his mouth.

Eventually, when he'd driven her out of her mind with his attention to her breasts, Sean moved down her midriff, kissing her stomach, tasting her navel. He went lower, until his lips brushed the elastic of her panties and his hot breaths pressed the silky fabric against the lips of her sex.

They were reaching the point of no return here. Hell, they were probably already past it. And Annie was absolutely desperate for him to tug that fabric away with his teeth and dive into her like a starving man would at a buffet.

Instead, he surprised her by kissing his way back up her body. Reaching her face, he brushed his mouth against hers, and slid his hand into her hair. "Second date…second base, right?"

She let out a shaky breath. "I don't remember the bases…but I kind of think we went around second and were sliding into third there."

"I'm an Irishman. What do I know about baseball?"

He kissed her again, so tenderly she knew he was about to stand up and end the interlude. Half wanting to bless him for having the strength to stand by *her* convictions—when she so obviously didn't—she also wanted to grab him by the hair and pull him back down.

"Annie," he murmured as he began to rise. "I didn't come here to seduce you into changing your mind. Let me take you out and we'll stick by our agreement." Reaching for her hand, he added, "Just be prepared. When I bring you back here on Sunday after our third date—at your parents' place—I won't be leaving for *many* hours."

His words weren't so much a statement as a promise, and it was emphasized by the sultry half smile on his mouth. It didn't exactly make the ache between her thighs go away, but did relieve the one in her head which had started the moment she'd realized he really was going to stop.

She couldn't think of what would happen after

Sunday. Where he'd go, whether she'd ever hear from him again.

That would turn the pounding behind her eyes into a full-blown migraine.

"Now go get dressed."

"Okay," she said, letting him pull her to her feet. His gaze locked on her bared breasts, the heat in them stopping her heart and almost sending her tumbling back to the couch. Then he reached for her robe and handed it to her.

Nuts.

"I know exactly what I'm wearing," she whispered as she tugged her bra back into place and donned the robe. Hoping she didn't still sound as thoroughly aroused as she felt, she forced a smile. "I'll only be a minute."

His eyebrows went up. "So the answering-the-door-in-the-robe wasn't really necessary?"

"Oh, it was necessary," she said over her shoulder as she strode across the small living room. "I was confused about whether we were going on the date you offered in the program, or to a nice restaurant. I just had to wait and see how you were dressed before I knew for sure."

"What program?" he asked.

But Annie didn't turn around to answer. It had taken sheer determination to stride away from him as if she'd gone back to normal just as easily and quickly as he obviously had. She wasn't up for trying to chat when her legs felt like two bunches of rubber bands, without strength or form. Pushing her bedroom door closed, she leaned back against it, taking the opportunity to suck in a few deep, shattered breaths.

It took about a minute, but her heart rate finally

returned to normal. Once it had, Annie moved fast. She grabbed her brush, fixed her hair, then touched up her makeup.

"Elegant," she told her reflection, going a bit heavier on the eye shadow. For a ball game, the soft beige would have been fine. A shadowy restaurant called for something more dramatic. At least, as dramatic as she could get in sixty seconds.

She finished getting ready quickly, going with the dark, glittery red dress. While she usually stuck with softer, spring colors, tonight she wanted to stand out, to be as vivid as a flame. To look like someone who should be on the arm of a man as good-looking as Sean.

Remembering the confusion in Sean's voice when he'd asked about the program, Annie grabbed the page she'd torn out. The comment he'd made about baseball a few minutes ago—not the sexual innuendo, but the actual game—made her wonder *why* he would offer a woman a date to a Cubs game. It just seemed so out of character.

Something wasn't adding up. Intending to ask him about it over dinner, Annie folded carefully folded the page and tucked it into her purse.

When she walked back into the other room five minutes after she'd left it, her clothes were changed, her pulse was back to normal, and her freshly changed panties were completely dry.

Though, if they stayed that way all evening, she'd be shocked.

"Okay, I'm…" Her words trailed off as she noticed Sean holding something curled up like a baby in his arms.

It was Wally. And he was *purring*.

Shock made her jaw drop. "You drugged him. Like

in that movie *Something About Mary*. He's *never* this friendly."

"Are you kidding? He's a big softie." He scratched the cat under his chin, and Wally rubbed his furry head against the man's hands. His very talented hands, as she knew well.

Maybe it wasn't so strange that Wally was being nice to someone else for the first time in his life. Sean's hands could make a grown woman purr…why not a cat?

Shaking off the memory of those hands on her body, she said, "He also sheds badly. Your jacket will be a mess."

Shrugging, Sean lowered the cat to the sofa, then began to pick the fur off his previously immaculate suit coat. Pushing his hands away, Annie did it for him, suddenly struck by the cozy intimacy of such an act. Like they were a regular couple, going out on a regular date.

It was…nice.

A little confused and suddenly feeling awkward, she stepped back. "That's better. I guess we're both ready."

He looked her up and down. "I didn't know women were capable of getting dressed so quickly."

"I shouldn't be. It's not like I wear clothes like this very often. But I'm a pro at yanking on a new shirt to replace one that's got baby formula or strained peas on it."

He grinned. "Hazards of the job."

"Yep. But it's nice to do something different. Now, at least if my mother asks me if you've taken me anywhere special, I can honestly say yes."

His grin faded, and she immediately regretted reminding him of how they'd met and why they were together. So much for being a normal couple. It had been lovely to pretend for a moment…but it wasn't true.

Maybe it was good to be reminded of that. She needed to remember that whether or not they had an official "third date"—and everything it entailed—this wasn't going to go anywhere. How could it? She knew almost *nothing* about this man. Not where he lived, where he worked. Not where he was headed after this weekend. She only knew how he affected her.

Isn't that enough? that reckless inner voice whispered. A fling with a gorgeous man was probably just what the sex doctor would order after the Blake fiasco.

It was definitely something to consider.

"Have you been telling your family about a new boyfriend?"

Annie jerked her head back, wondering if he saw the guilt in her eyes. She quickly glanced around the apartment, looking for some telltale sign that she'd been seeing someone recently. Blake had only ever been inside her place a few times, so she had no idea what it could be.

"Because, I imagine they think he's someone special if you're bringing him home for a family event like this."

Of course. He wasn't overly suspicious, just asking a natural question. "Uh…yeah."

"Do I have a name?" He sounded resigned. "Please say it's not somethin' stupid like Pierce or Todd."

"Blake," she whispered.

"Ugh."

"I haven't given any details about looks, personality, age or anything," she quickly added. "They just know—er—*believe,* that I've been seeing someone."

And thank God for that. Maybe not telling her family anything about Blake—including the fact that he had a son—had been an indication that, deep inside, Annie had known something was wrong with the relationship. That same instinct might have kept her from actually having sex with him.

So perhaps she ought to give her instincts a break. They'd served her well in that much, at least.

"I should have known, given the mumbling you were doing at the auction the other night."

She'd forgotten about that.

"All right, I suppose we can work with that. But, oh, woman, did you intentionally set yourself up to have your brothers harass you? Why on earth did you pick such a girly-man name?"

She bit her lip, preventing a quick laugh. Oh, would she love to see Blake's expression if he heard those words coming out of this incredibly hot man's mouth.

No. Actually, she wouldn't. She never wanted to see that man again, never wanted to think about him or even remember she'd once let herself believe she was falling for him.

He was the past. Who might be in her future, she couldn't say. But for her present—for this weekend—there was only Sean.

"Just a lapse in judgment," she admitted softly, both to him and to herself. "It was a simple mistake, one I need to forget about."

Starting right now.

5

SEAN HAD BEEN grabbing taxis while in Chicago for this trip. But since he had wanted Annie to get the full "auction date" package, he had hired a limo for the evening. When they walked out of her apartment building and she saw the long, shiny black vehicle standing at the curb, her eyes widened in delight.

"Thank you," she murmured as he escorted her to the door, where the driver stood waiting. "You went all out for tonight, when you didn't have to. I'm sure you spent way too much money."

He could certainly afford it, but didn't say that. Annie hadn't asked him about his job, how he lived, what he lived on. He wanted to keep it that way a little while longer. "Who says I didn't have to? You put out a lot of money at the auction…"

"For this weekend," she clarified as they got into the car. She slid across the leather seat, making room for him to sit beside her. As he did, her long, slim leg brushed against his, and Sean had to tug his stare away by sheer force of will. He hardly heard her as she continued. "And you're paying me back in full by helping me out with my family." She waved a hand, gesturing at the inside of the car. "This…was definitely over and above the call of duty."

His smile wolfish, he asked, "Does that mean you

want to go back upstairs and give me a piece of pizza for date two?"

Laughing softly, she shook her head. "Not on your life."

During the ride to the restaurant, she checked out every inch of the car, peeking into the minibar, tapping her nail against the rim of a glass to test the crystal. She didn't go so far as to open the sunroof and pop up through it, but otherwise, seemed to enjoy every typical bit of a standard limo ride. He suspected she'd never been in one.

Sean wasn't the limo type. He much preferred taxis to get around cities he was visiting, or his own cars when he was at home. But it was fun to watch her. Considering the small apartment, her simple clothes, her understated jewelry and her salt-of-the-earth background, he suspected Annie didn't indulge in luxuries very often.

He liked indulging her. And was glad to be in the position to be able to do it.

It certainly hadn't always been that way.

Sean had grown up with money, though his father hadn't believed in spoiling his son and heir. But he'd never lacked for anything. When he'd lit out on his own, however, things had changed. He hadn't been broke, but the trust fund his paternal grandmother had left him had only gone so far. He'd nursed it along, doing the starving-student thing—hostels, backpacking—while figuring out what he wanted to do with his life. Still, the fund had grown dangerously small.

Then he'd figured out what he was really good at— charming people and making deals—and had begun to make serious money.

He'd never looked back.

"So where are we going?"

He named the restaurant, which she hadn't heard of. That didn't surprise him. He wasn't taking her to one of the typical well-known establishments in town. This was the kind of place that only locals frequented, since it sat atop a private condominium high-rise. Sean had stumbled across it on a previous visit and knew its ambiance, location near the water and outstanding food were perfect for tonight.

As nice as the restaurant was, he did have one regret about its location. It wasn't very far, meaning their intimate car ride would go by much too quickly. So he couldn't even *think* about trying to introduce her to one of the nicest perks of being chauffeured—hot, steamy car sex.

Second date, remember?

"I could get used to this," she finally said as she sank back into the seat, closing her eyes. Her long lashes brushed her high cheekbones. Sean suddenly had the urge to kiss her there, to brush his lips against those closed lids, then work his way across her temple and over to her fragile earlobes.

He resisted. They had a whole evening to get through, then an entire weekend surrounded by her family. He needed to get a grip on himself—on the desire that had been coursing through him since he'd first set eyes on Annie Monday night. For a man used to taking things slow, anticipating and savoring the very best things in life, his hunger for her was maddening.

When they arrived at the restaurant, Sean tipped the maître d' to get the table he wanted. It was a very private one in an alcove beside windows that overlooked the lake far below them. The dull green water appeared crystalline from this height and glimmered under the last rays of the setting summer sun.

"Beautiful," she murmured.

She was. The view was all right, too.

"You can see forever. It's hard to believe the ocean is bigger than this. Not that I'd know."

He raised a brow. "You don't mean…"

"Nope. I've never seen it." Her jaw stiffened. "But I intend to. In fact, I intend to see *all* of them."

That would be a good trick, given the temperatures in the Arctic. But he had noted her resolute tone and wasn't about to argue with her. This delicate, sweet-faced woman had serious will. She'd certainly proven the lengths she'd go to in order to get what she wanted…like a weekend with *him*.

Still, the idea that she'd never even traveled to either side of her own country stunned him. Maybe it was because the width of *his* country could be traversed in a single day.

Or maybe it was because he had such a hard time seeing her in that world. How could this strong-willed woman—who'd gone after what she wanted with both hands—have come from a family who had never even noticed her hunger for something more?

He was still shaking his head over it when the waiter brought the wine he'd ordered. As he sampled it, doing the typical wine-opening dance with the tuxedoed waiter, he realized Annie was watching closely, wearing a tiny frown.

"What's wrong?" he asked when they were again alone.

"Nothing." She shook her head slowly, then admitted, "It's just…I don't know how this weekend is going to go over."

"Because we're practically strangers and have to pretend to be intimately involved?"

Her cheeks colored a little, and he knew she was thinking of the intimacies they'd shared at her apartment.

"Okay. So we are intimately involved," he conceded. *Though not intimately enough.* "But we haven't known each other long."

"And you're very different."

Since he'd just been thinking about her background, he knew where she was heading. "You mean from your family."

She nodded.

"Are you saying I'm not exactly the 'bring him home to meet the parents' type of bloke?"

She shook her head. "I shouldn't have said anything. You'll be fine. Even if you aren't what I'd expected."

"What were you expecting?"

She lifted her glass of wine, sipped, raised an appreciative brow, then replied. "Not an Irishman, for one thing. From the bio, I thought I'd be getting some nice boy from a blue-collar neighborhood who grew up watching *E.R.* and decided to become a paramedic."

"A *what?*"

She eyed him quizzically. "A paramedic. That's what you are, right? Or, do I have the terminology wrong? Are you an EMT?"

"Annie, I haven't got any idea what you're talking about."

Hesitating for one moment, as if making sure his shock was genuine, she reached for her purse and pulled out a folded piece of paper. "I grabbed this earlier. I had the feeling something was a little strange. Read it for yourself," she said, shoving the page at him. "It says nothing about you being an Irishman...just about you being a rescue worker."

Sean grabbed the page, read it intently, and shook his head in utter bewilderment. Because the words beneath his picture made absolutely no sense. "That's not me."

"It's you," she insisted.

"I meant the *description*. I'm not that man." Unable to figure out what the hell was going on, he frowned, "I know I sent the correct information, that I'm a…" How had he worded it? "An international, traveling businessman."

Annie's eyes widened and she grabbed the sheet out of his hands. She flipped it over, scanned the words beneath the photo of Bachelor Number Nineteen, and said, "Aha! Is *this* what you wrote?"

Sean read the bio. *European businessman. Worldly. Loves travel, women and playing.* Yeah, that sounded like what he'd said. After all, putting "paid escort for rich women" hadn't sounded right. "Consultant making difficult deals for international companies" hadn't either. So he'd gone a little overboard with the adjectives that might appeal to the bachelor-auction type.

"Yes, it is. Somebody obviously mixed up the biographies." A small smile widened his lips as he caught sight of the picture above *his* bio. "I wonder how that Jake guy liked being mistaken for a…for *me*."

"Let's just hope the woman who shelled out twenty-five grand wasn't dying for a guy with an accent."

He was silent for a moment, considering, then suddenly laughed out loud. Good God, the women who'd bid in such a frenzy over the laid-back paramedic… Was it possible they had been tipped off about what to look for in *Sean's* bio, and that's what had driven the amount up to such an extreme figure?

If so, he *really* felt bad for the other man. Boy, was

he going to have some explaining to do to the woman who'd shelled out that much money to be with him.

Sean, however, had no such worries. Annie had bid on him for no reason other than the ones she'd already shared. Which was pretty damned honest and refreshing, considering the dealings he'd had with women for the past several years. "Well, then, now I don't feel so bad about being outsold."

Annie sipped her drink again, her soft blue eyes gleaming in the low light. The sun had gone down, the interior of the restaurant descending into shadow and candlelight. The golden flicker of the flame picked up the highlights in her long, blond hair, and emphasized the fragility of her jaw, the slenderness of her throat.

The woman was completely, utterly feminine. Every inch of her was soft and perfectly defined. And so close to being his, he could almost taste her.

Peaches.

"You know," she said, interrupting his lazy, hungry musings, "I can't help thinking about how different things might have been if the program hadn't been messed up."

Oh, she had no idea. "Me, too."

"I was genuinely attracted to your picture. But your *real* bio might have made me try harder for one of the earlier guys—the nice guy, hero types."

"You saying I'm not a nice guy?" When she gasped in embarrassment, he chuckled, letting her know he wasn't serious. "Kidding. I know what you meant."

She gave him a little glare, reminding him of how she responded to teasing. Then she continued. "I mean, an all-American rescue worker would probably have scored points with my family. I don't think I would have read about an international traveling businessman

who loved women and considered him a suitable match
for a freckle-nosed day care center operator from Green
Springs, Illinois."

He said nothing for a second, knowing she hadn't
been fishing for compliments. She was just open and
honest…the only way the woman appeared to know
how to be.

He could be no less.

"And what a loss that would have been," he
murmured, meaning it with every fiber of his being.

She licked her lips, falling silent, as if she was replaying his words. Hearing, too, the ones he didn't say.

That he was glad they'd met, glad she'd chosen him.
And very anxious to see what came next.

All the same thoughts echoing in his own head.
None spoken, but there just the same.

"I'm glad we met, Sean," she finally whispered.

"So am I." He reached across the table and brushed
her fingers with his, lacing them together atop the crisp
white tablecloth. "Whoever messed up that program
might have done me a terrific favor."

"I think they did me a favor, too." She kept her right
hand where it was, touching his, but lifted her wineglass with her left. Raising it in salute, she added,
"Here's to the person who screwed up."

Sean didn't hesitate to join in her toast. "May he be
in heaven a half-hour before the devil knows he's dead."

BY THREE O'CLOCK Friday afternoon, Sean knew there
was no way he was going to be able to wait until the
next morning to see Annie again. Maybe if they were
going to head off to a romantic hotel for their weekend
holiday, he'd be able to stand it. But the thought that
they'd be surrounded by her nosy, overprotective

family for two days, without a moment alone, made the prospect of a getaway a whole lot less appealing.

Considering how much he'd enjoyed her company last night, he just wanted to spend more time with her. Hearing her laugh, watching her eyes light up when she smiled. Seeing the amazement on her face when she tried something new—like the limo ride or the caviar he'd persuaded her to sample. Their relaxed, low-key after-dinner walk along the water to see the stars had ended one of the most pleasant evenings he'd ever enjoyed in this city.

His impatience had everything to do with how much he'd enjoyed being with her…and nothing to do with him dying for that third date—and its conclusion.

Well, *almost* nothing.

Yes, he enjoyed spending time with her. But he had to admit, after having her in his arms—tasting her, caressing her before they'd left for dinner, then gently kissing her again when he'd escorted her to her door late last night—he was *dying* to make love to the woman.

And he would.

He'd have her, get the wanting out of his system and move on. He had places to go, jobs to complete, and staying in Chicago after this weekend was out of the question.

So, why did the thought of leaving her so soon suddenly made his fists clench? But the fact that it did merely reiterated his need to get going, to move on, stick to his mantra that it wasn't good to stay in one place for too long. Nor to form connections that would last more than a few weeks at most.

"Time to go, mate," he muttered. *After* he'd had her.

That certainty made the desperation to see her even

more frustrating. He didn't want to waste the little bit of time they had left by twiddling his thumbs in his hotel room all evening. And another solitary jack-off session in the shower would do absolutely nothing to cure him of his insane need for the sexy blonde.

Though, honestly, given the way he could still see her sprawled on her back on the couch—her bare breasts jutting toward him in welcome, her entire body shivering with need—he was going to have to do *something*.

So see her.

Easier said than done, since she was working tonight. He *had* to wait.

"Hell," he muttered. He was no good at waiting.

Giving up any pretense that he was *going* to wait, he started calling Annie's cell number, which he'd programmed into his. He had a good excuse. After their conversation at dinner last night, he'd begun thinking about the ordeal ahead. Her comment about how much easier things would be if he'd truly been some kind of blue-collar rescue worker had put him on edge, made him wonder about this charade they were going to try to pull on her family.

It had sounded so simple at first. Now, though, the whole thing seemed more daunting. Maybe because he knew Annie enough to know how much this meant to her. And because he already liked her enough to feel the pressure of wanting it to go well.

Whatever the reason, he didn't want to screw this up. Meaning they *should* work on their story. If they'd been dating for two months, he'd at least know the woman's middle name and the way she took her coffee.

In any normal situation, after two months, he'd damn sure know her favorite sexual positions and her most erogenous zones, too. But that might be pushing it for a simple weekend with the folks.

The phone rang and rang, but Annie didn't answer. Remembering that she said she rarely did while at work, he waited until six, figuring she'd turn the phone on then, even if she was working late. But still nothing.

Finally, at eight, when she still hadn't responded, Sean began to worry. She had joked about being surrounded by babies tonight, but he hadn't taken her seriously. Day care centers didn't stay open late at night. He'd figured she just had meetings or paperwork to take care of. So there was no reason for her to remain unreachable.

Annie's comment about her family expecting her to turn up violated or murdered had been ringing a little too loudly in his ears for comfort.

He'd lost her card, but remembered the name of the center, and the area where it was located, if not the actual address. So he *could* have tried information for her work number. But some impulse—half worry, half impatience to see her—drove him from the hotel. Hailing a cab, he had it take him to Lincoln Park.

Fortunately, they only had to drive about twenty blocks before he saw the brightly colored Baby Daze sign in front of a small, well-kept brick building.

"There," he said, pointing the place out to the driver. Parked outside the front door was a green minivan.

Good Lord, no wonder she'd liked the limo.

Waving the driver on, Sean walked to the front door, cupped his hands around his face and peeked inside. What he saw relieved him—since Annie sat there, safe and sound. But it also terrified him.

Because she was not alone. She sat on a child-size chair, in the middle of a mob of chattery, cookie-clutching, milk-mustached kids.

Every one of whom began to scream when they saw him watching them through the glass-plated door.

ON TWO FRIDAY NIGHTS a month, Baby Daze held a "Mom And Dad's Dinner Out" event. Three members of the staff would work late, keeping no more than twelve children—age three and up—until nine o'clock. The event had proved so popular, they now had a waiting list stretching into next fall.

It was one of the little services that had helped make Baby Daze such an early and decisive success. Things were going so well that Annie suspected she might be able to replenish that emergency savings account within a few months, rather than the year it probably would have taken her before.

"A strange man!" someone shouted. The chorus was quickly taken up by all the children. "A man, a man, a man!"

Startled into dropping the wet naps she'd been using to wipe off a dozen pair of sticky hands, Annie jerked her attention toward the locked front door, toward which twelve little arms were already pointing. She immediately recognized the surprised—uncomfortable-looking—face of Sean Murphy.

Willing her racing heart to still, she called for Tara to come finish supervising the kids' bedtime snack, then approached the door. Unlocking it, she stepped out into the summer evening, wondering if the warmth she felt was simply because her body was adjusting to leaving the air-conditioned room. Or because, as always, she just found Sean Murphy so incredibly *hot*.

"Hi."

"Sorry. I didn't mean to intrude. You weren't answering your cell phone and I got a little worried."

He was worried about her. When her family acted that way, it infuriated her. But Sean? Well, Annie couldn't prevent a pleased shiver at the realization that he'd been thinking so much about her. As she had him.

"I was running late this morning and I forgot my phone. It's still on the charger at my place."

"Ahh." He looked past her, into the room, where the kids were cleaning up their snack tables, licking tiny crumbs off the tips of their fingers. They'd already exhausted their curiosity about the stranger at the door, who they obviously figured was *not* a bad guy since Miss Annie was standing outside talking to him. Graham cracker crumbs were much more interesting.

"I'd better go. I didn't mean to intrude."

"Why were you trying to reach me?"

"I thought maybe we should work on our story before we got to your parents' place tomorrow."

"Our story?"

"You know…how we—you and *Blake*—met. That type of thing. We never really covered that last night."

Annie felt the blood rush out of her face, and she leaned back against the door. *How they met.* God, she did *not* want to think about how she'd met Blake. Especially *here,* where her guilt and humiliation were at their highest level.

"I'm sure we can work it out on the drive tomorrow," she muttered, already regretting having to wait until then to spend more time with him.

Hearing a shout behind them, Annie spun around and peered through the window. Dylan McFee had just tackled Jessie Sims, trying to steal a toy he wanted. Tara leapt into the fray, as did Ellen, the other worker who'd volunteered for tonight's shift.

"I should go, you're busy."

"Yeah," she whispered. Then, looking back at him and seeing the amusement dancing in those sexy eyes, she found herself saying, "There's a restaurant up the street. Maybe you could go have a drink or something and wait for me to finish up? Then we can…talk?"

Holding her breath, she couldn't help smiling in pure relief when he nodded his agreement. "What time?"

"Pick-up is no later than nine. Someone will be late and apologetic. But I should be able to get out of here by nine-thirty, nine-forty-five at the latest."

"Perfect. I'll see you then." He cast one more glance at the melee going on inside, wearing a childless-single man grimace so pained it made her chuckle. Then he strode down the block, his thick, black, unbound hair flowing loosely over his shoulders. Lord, why was the sight of one man's hair enough to send all the strength from her legs and set all her feminine parts tingling?

She shook off the reaction, needing to get through the rest of the work night.

Once back inside, she immediately saw the excitement on Tara's face. It was echoed by the curiosity on Ellen's. But they were all too busy getting the children ready for their parents' arrival to talk about it. By the time the last ones *did* arrive, at nine-twenty-eight, Annie had already sent Ellen home and was just waiting for an explosion of questions from Tara.

She got it as soon as the door swung shut behind the last child and his stammering, apologetic parents.

"That was him, right? Damn, I didn't get a good look."

Rushing around to pick up the few remaining toys scattered in the room, Annie nodded. "It was him."

"What did he want?" Looking fierce, her friend

snapped, "He'd better not be bailing out on you, not the night before you're supposed to go away together!"

Fierce, fiery and flamboyant. That described Tara.

"No, he's not. He just wants to get together and make sure we have our stories straight."

"Smart move." Tara grinned. "You might want to *do* him, too, just to make sure you're totally comfortable with each other. Or at least kiss him, because, you know, if he's a sucky kisser, you don't want to be surprised into gagging or something."

She hadn't told Tara about her two dates with Sean. Though she usually told her friend everything, this whole thing was just too new—too private—to be girl-talked about.

"*Doing* him is out of the question," she said. *At least until Sunday*. "And he's definitely *not* a sucky kisser."

It was only when she heard a smothered male cough behind her that she realized they were no longer alone. Casting Tara a glare that promised extreme retribution, she slowly turned around and saw Sean standing inside the door. He'd probably heard every word she'd said.

Unfortunately, the tables in Baby Daze were much smaller than the ones at the hotel had been. So there was no ducking beneath one of them to escape the humiliation of the moment.

"Door was unlocked," Sean explained, his eyes twinkling. Yeah, he'd definitely overheard.

"That's fine, we were just finishing up," Tara said as she strode toward him, extending her hand. "I'm Tara. I was at the auction, too. So I know who you are, meaning, uh, if you try any nasty stuff, I'll turn the cops on you like a hunter loosing his dogs."

"Go away, Tara," Annie mumbled, not even sparing her friend a glance.

"Well, then, now that you've been warned, it was nice to meet you." Tara gave Sean a big smile, as if she hadn't just threatened him with bodily harm. Before she left, however, she turned back to Annie. "You're right. The earring is way sexy." Then she walked out the door.

Annie followed her out, avoiding the moment when she'd have to face Sean and see the laughter on his face. Locking the door, she flipped off the main lights, which killed the sign outside, as well as the overhead fluorescents in the building. Finally, when she had no more reason to delay, she turned around to face the music.

The large playroom in which they stood was plunged nearly into darkness, remaining dimly lit by the spillover from her office and the kitchen. No longer bright and welcoming, the room became a shapeless cave of shadows, interrupted here and there by the sunny yellow of the doll house or the colorful plastic balls piled in the enormous ball pit the kids loved to play in.

"So I'm not a sucky kisser, eh?" He'd moved close—close enough that she could feel his warmth, though she hadn't spotted him as her eyes adjusted to the change in lighting. "I'm relieved to know I don't make you gag."

Dropping her head, Annie sighed and closed her eyes.

He touched her chin, brushing his fingertips across her skin as if savoring its softness, then tugged her head up and murmured, "But why, may I ask, is 'doing me' out of the question?"

"You weren't supposed to hear that."

"The question remains."

"Third date, remember? We're practically strangers."

That was true, but she had to be honest with herself.

She already felt sure she knew his character very well…and she wanted him with a desperation that made her burn down to her core.

"I'm holding you to the third date promise," he said. "And I'm here to remedy the strangers issue. Even you won't be able to argue that for much longer…"

Argue? Was she arguing? No, she was just putting up a few minor defenses, knowing that if she didn't, she'd be throwing her arms around his shoulders, begging him to get to know her in the most elemental way possible.

She had juice and graham crackers in the kitchen of the center. Did that count as a date?

As if knowing just how far to push her, how to keep her senses heightened and her defenses down, Sean stepped away and looked around. "Ready for our little chat?"

"Here?" she yelped, startled that he had stepped away without kissing her. She wondered if he could read her disappointment.

"I'd know something about your work, wouldn't I?"

The real Blake hadn't known anything about Annie's work, beyond the fact that a day care center was a great place to hit on single women. And that maybe, if he was lucky, he could both bang the owner and get a discount on his son's care.

Not that she was about to tell *him* that.

"So you own this place?"

"I do. I don't actually own the building, but have a long-term lease which allowed me to make all the renovations."

"And you're obviously successful."

"I think so. Certainly more than anybody ever expected me to be."

"What did they expect?" he asked. Walking around

the room while he waited for her to answer, he examined the scrawled crayon drawings, side-by-side with colorful framed fairy-tale paintings on the wall.

"My parents were certain my degree in early child-hood education was preparing me to be a wonderful mother." Her tone could have held a mouthful of sand and not been any more dry.

"They had no idea you were taking off?"

Frustrated, Annie ran her fingers through her blond hair to smooth it. "Of course they knew. I'd been saying for *years* that I planned to go, to see the world, to live on my own."

"They just didn't believe it," he murmured.

"Exactly. Because they *also* know I really do want the things they want for me—marriage, family. I just don't want them on their terms."

He stiffened the tiniest bit, like any determined bachelor would when confronted with terrifying words like marriage and family.

Annie took no offense. Since the moment she'd met Sean Murphy, she'd had no illusions about the kind of man she was taking home to meet the folks—a worldly one who in no way fit into her life. Not in the long term, at least.

But for this weekend—especially after their third date—all bets were off.

"Families always seem to want things on their own terms," he admitted, almost in a whisper, as if the darkness of the place indicated a need for quiet.

Realizing that there was no normal-size chair out here for him to sit on—just little plastic ones that would never hold his weight—she said, "I need to go lock up my office. Why don't we go talk in there."

He followed her, taking the seat she pointed to,

directly across from her desk. It was fine for her average visitor—the concerned parent checking the place out for the first time, the worker applying for a job. But it was nowhere near suitable for the big, broad man who seemed to fill up the entire office with his presence.

Sean wasn't dressed in jeans and a button-down shirt tonight, or a ridiculously expensive-looking suit like he'd worn to dinner. Instead, he wore tailored black trousers and a tight, short-sleeved gray shirt, cut like a T-shirt but made of some shimmering fabric that said it *hadn't* come out of a plastic bag marked Jockey.

And she was in the usual khaki pants and a blue, stained Baby Daze golf shirt.

Who said they didn't look just like a matched pair?

Who cares? It's one weekend!

"It's obvious just by looking around that you've made a success of it," he finally said as he glanced around the office, noting the framed certificates and licenses on the wall. "Your family must concede that much."

"You'd think."

"Well, then, we'll just have to convince them that you've at least done well with your choices in men."

That caused her to snort out loud.

He leaned back in the chair, kicking his long legs out in front of him, and crossed his big arms over his chest. "Speaking of which, what do I do for a living?"

"I didn't say."

He nodded, thinking about it. "How about…mechanic?" His eyes twinkled, and she remembered their first conversation.

Her head tilted back in challenge. "Know what a socket wrench looks like?"

"Good point. Uh…pediatrician?"

She smirked. "I saw the way you looked at the kids."

"I like children," he protested, sounding indignant…but not terribly honest.

"En brochette?"

His deep, throaty laugh sent a tingle of sensation racing through her. She *liked* the man's laugh. And his smile. And the way those eyes lit up when he was amused.

"Busted. Is that the word? I suppose I did see the little monsters and immediately wonder if I needed to don protective gear to come in and rescue you."

She frowned. "They're adorable."

"They're sticky."

"They're loving," she insisted.

"They're loud."

"They're loyal."

"They're *short*."

"Oh, all right," she said, grinning too much to keep up the ridiculous game of one-upsmanship. "They're all of the above. But I love them just the same."

"I saw that," he murmured, eyeing her intently, his expression almost—tender—if that made any sense. Especially given his obvious disinterest in children. Then that strong chin went up and he said, "Of course, that's everyone else's children. I don't imagine my own—*if* I ever get around to having any, which I sincerely doubt—would be sticky, loud or short."

At that, Annie leaned back in her chair and chortled. "You're a pompous one, aren't you?"

Shock unhinged his jaw. "I'm no such thing."

"A little pompous," she clarified. "And spoiled."

"Maybe once," he admitted. "Not anymore."

Their stares locked across her desk, and she sensed the intensity in the man. He hadn't wanted to talk about his past, beyond mentioning that he'd been raised in Ireland. There was a story there—most definitely. But he'd put up walls around himself, using his easy charm and amazing good looks to keep anyone from surmounting them.

What, she wondered, would await a woman who managed to get to the other side?

"We still haven't settled on my occupation," he said, clearing his throat and breaking their intense visual connection. As if he knew she'd been trying to figure him out. "Hmm…stunt man? Body double for Brad Pitt?"

She snorted. "He *wishes* people believed he had a body like yours."

Then she got serious, knowing they really had to nail this down, if only so she could hammer the details into her own head tonight. The last thing she needed was to get caught in a lie by her family, who'd be all over any prevarication like Dylan McFee had been all over Jessie Sims to get that toy.

"Let's keep it simple. You're a businessman." That, according to his *correct* bio, was true. She hated to draw him much further into her lies, though the mischief in his expression said he was having fun with the whole charade. "The closer we stick to the truth, the better. And that *is* the truth, right?"

He shifted in the uncomfortable chair. "More or less. I'm a consultant. But businessman will do." Moving on, he asked, "Where did we meet?"

Annie's hands clenched into fists beneath the desk, and she willed her jaw not to clench in instinctive anger. So much for sticking close to the truth. She didn't even want to pretend to have met this man the way she'd met the real Blake—here, at work, where she *so* should have known better.

"Dating service?"

He rolled his eyes. "Pathetic. How about a blind date?"

"And that's *not* pathetic?"

He frowned, thinking it over. "Party?"

"Fine."

She felt like they were negotiating a contract, rather than establishing a relationship. And suddenly saw that he probably would be a very good businessman.

He confirmed it by running down a list of questions she never even would have thought to ask. Her favorite color, flower, movie and musician. Her political leanings, ambitions, where she went to school. How she took her coffee, her favorite ice cream. Ticklish spots.

She told him one. But she left the other out altogether. He'd come close to discovering it on her couch yesterday evening. Close...but not quite. And if he ever discovered that one, they'd be a whole lot more involved than two people planning to pull a little scam on her family this weekend should be.

All the details he wanted to know were minor, but certainly things a couple would know about each other. Cake or pie? Chocolate or vanilla? He filed each detail away, occasionally volunteering an opinion on her preferences—*how can you prefer apple pie over Crème Brûlée?*—but quickly moving along.

These were all details they could have talked about over dinner last night, in the typical, second date, get-to-know-you manner. Instead, they'd laughed about the program mix-up, speculating on the wealthy woman's reaction to getting Jake the paramedic rather than the international businessman. He'd harassed her into tasting caviar, though not escargot, and she'd intentionally asked for a doggie bag, just to see how he'd react.

She should have known. Sean had at first grinned, then raised an arrogant brow and barked at the waiter when the guy had been snitty about it.

Through all that, they'd somehow skipped over all the basic chitchat, as if already so comfortable with one another, none of it had mattered. Until now, when they realized it *did,* at least as far as her family was concerned.

The conversation continued in that vein for a few minutes, until he matter-of-factly asked, "Do you sleep in the nude?"

"What?"

"It's a fair question."

"No, it isn't," she said, part of her dying to tell him and part of her knowing she'd rather *show* him, instead. "My family is not going to ask you what I wear to bed, because my father would probably toss you out of the house if you answered."

"Old-fashioned."

"Very."

"We have a lot in common."

"Next question?"

"You didn't answer the last one."

She glared. *"Next question."*

"What size is your bed? I didn't even get a peek into your room yesterday."

Groaning as she realized the serious part of their conversation was over, she leaned across her desk and badly answered him. "It's big. Queen size."

And usually very empty. Wally generally slept sprawled out, taking up three-fourths of the mattress, leaving Annie clinging to the edge.

"I probably *should* see it," he said, sounding

entirely innocent for a man trying to maneuver his way into her bedroom.

Maneuver? So not necessary. Given how she'd been feeling about him—hot and attracted the first night, frankly interested the next, and comfortable and amused now—all he'd probably have to do is *ask*.

They'd spent more than an hour together, talking, laughing, flirting. This *so* counted as a date.

"Don't you agree that I should at least…take a peek?"

Inside her chest, her heart did that funny fluttering thing again. And her thighs clenched. "Why?"

"Well, we're dating, aren't we? I'm a gentleman, and I'd be sure to escort you to your door. So it's likely I'd have at least gotten a glimpse at your bedroom."

"You get along with Wally. That's proof that you're in my life."

"Back to the previous question then. What do you wear when you crawl into that big bed with just your cat for company?"

Unable to resist, she told him in a throaty whisper, "A red silk nightie."

Lie, lie, lie. She usually wore a long T-shirt to bed. But she at least *had* a red nightie. She'd bought it at an after-Valentine's Day sale last winter, determined to have worn it for *somebody* before the next time the fat baby with the arrows flew around.

Maybe it'll actually happen. Now. Tonight.

A muscle flexed in Sean's jaw, and his eyes narrowed the tiniest bit. That, and the almost inaudible hiss of his indrawn breath, was his only reaction. "Long or short?"

Mmm…she suspected he was very long. He certainly had felt that way pressed against her yesterday.

And he most definitely had been in her erotic dreams of the night before.

Annie's breaths merged together, tripping over each other as they rushed from her lungs. She'd forgotten about the dreams until this minute. Now they were replaying themselves in her thoughts in full, glorious Technicolor, reminding her that she'd awakened at four in the morning, her body quivering as an intense orgasm shook her from her sleep.

Annie swallowed, trying to force the images away. At least long enough to answer the question he had *really* been asking.

The shadow of a smile on his lips told her he knew what had been going through her mind. "I meant the gown."

"I knew that," she insisted, sounding about as convincing as one of the kids trying to talk his way into another cookie.

"Of course you did."

"It's…" She tried to remember. The thing had been hanging on a padded silk hanger in her closet since the day she'd bought it. "Long!" Definitely long. She thought.

"What shade?"

"Shade?"

"Ruby red?" he asked, the voice so silky, the eyes intense. "Scarlet? Garnet? Is it the soft blush of a rosebud, or the wickedness of a fierce explosion of fire?"

Oh, God. The man painted pictures with his words. Pictures that formed entire scenarios in her brain.

Annie's whole body quivered, racing to process the sensations battering every inch of her. Breasts tingling and heavy against her shirt, nipples hard and jutting out in demand, arms shaking with the need to twine them around his neck and draw him to her. Every inch of her was affected.

Beneath the desk, her thighs quivered. The fierce explosion of fire he mentioned had erupted between them and it clawed at her, demanding attention. She was aroused and wet, her sex as aware and ready as if she'd been touched by his hands, rather than only his voice. As crazy as it sounded, if he kept on talking like that, her body was going to explode as unexpectedly as it had during her dreams the night before, just from the sultry sound of his whisper.

"Sean…"

He stared at her, certainty of her reaction washing off him, and for the briefest moment, she thought he was going to act on that certainty. To end the waiting, reach out, take her hand, and tug her across the desk. He'd tear her clothes off, set her on the edge of the desk and step between her shaking thighs. He'd fill her as she hadn't ever been filled. And then, maybe, they'd both be able to think again.

Instead, he did something even more shocking. He slowly rose from his chair and cleared his throat. "Well, I guess I have all I need."

To do what? The closet romance-novel reader inside her supplied a sudden, hopeful answer—*to ravish me? Right here? Right now?*

He didn't say that. Instead, with a few simple words, he deflated her, confused her.

And completely infuriated her.

"So I suppose we should say goodnight."

6

SEAN HAD TO GET OUT of here, now, while—as the old movies said—the getting was good. Judging by the flash of anger in Annie's pretty blue eyes, the "getting" might *not* be good in a few more moments. Because she looked to be building up a head of steam to tell him off. Call him a tease—or worse.

It was his own fault.

Although he'd intended tonight to be strictly about getting the information he needed, and getting an Annie fix to last him until their trip tomorrow, he'd found himself heading down a very dangerous path with her. One that saw them both veer off the main road of slow, casual friendship they should be on. And completely in sexual desire territory.

What kind of lackwit would ask her questions about what she wore to bed, and how big her bed was?

If he actually planned to *do* something about it, that'd be one thing. But he didn't. He'd promised her a third date. And tonight—despite how much he'd like to bend the rules and call it one—didn't count.

Besides, Sean was enjoying this new relationship, the strangeness of being with a woman without the pressures of expectation. He still didn't want to rush things. Though, if he didn't get out of here—now—he was not only going to rush things, he was going to set a new land record for getting a woman naked. Then another one for being inside her before either one of them could even think the words "we shouldn't," much less actually say them.

He glanced at his watch, noting now long they'd been talking. It was nearly eleven. They'd been completely lost to time, separated from the world outside. "We should go. It's getting pretty late. We've got a long day ahead of us tomorrow."

Staring at him, her eyes widened in shock, Annie collapsed back in her chair.

Don't. Please don't. If she said it—if she put the words out there between them, words like, "Why the hell aren't you tearing my clothes off by now?"—he'd lose all control. He'd have to have her right here in her place of business—a day care center, which should, for any single man, be about as erotic as a convent. But which, at this moment, would serve as well as a five-star hotel with a turned-down, silk-sheeted bed.

Finally, after a long, silent moment, she gave a brief nod and rose. If her chair flew back under her desk with a little more force than he'd expected, he wasn't going to call her on it. Or ask her what was wrong.

He *knew* what was wrong. He was a damned idiot, that's what was wrong. A fool who'd always insisted on opening his biggest present last on his birthday, who still ate every vegetable on his plate before allowing himself to savor the main course. Who'd always believed the best things in life were sweetened when you had to wait for them.

Waiting might heighten the excitement. But he wasn't sure his heart could *take* any more excitement when it came to what was going to happen between him and Annie.

"Too late, you blew it, dumb arse," he muttered as he left her office. She might have been hot and interested. Now she was *not* and angry.

Sean walked down the short hallway into the large main room, passing closed doors marked Nursery and Big Kids Only! The whole place remained shadowy and silent. What little illumination there was began to disappear as Annie turned off her office light. She closed the door behind her, then reached around the corner into another room to flip one more switch.

Now there was nothing but darkness, broken only by the redness of the Exit signs and the glimmer of moonlight easing through the front windows. That was still enough, however, for him to make out the gleam of Annie's blond hair as she approached. And, as she drew closer, the glitter of her eyes.

Her angry eyes.

"Annie…"

"I'm almost ready," she said as she checked the thermostat. "Feel free to leave."

"I'm not leavin' you to walk outside into the night by yourself." The day care center was in a commercial area, not a residential one. When he'd gone down the block for a drink, he'd noticed every building between here and there had been closed and dark, those in the opposite direction appearing much the same.

"Suit yourself," she said. "But you don't have to. I mean, I know it's not like you *want* to be here."

Hearing her frustration, and the echo of his own, deep inside his mind, Sean suddenly gave up his resistance. He wasn't going to be able to leave things like *this*. Not a chance could he have her going home thinking he didn't want her.

But before he could say anything—like, "Let's save

time in the morning by just going back to your place
for the night"—he felt something slam into his chest.
Something small, and, while lightweight, it still stung.

"What the bloody hell…"

Another colorful object zoomed out of the darkness.
This time, he reflexively reached up and grabbed it out
of the air, quickly realizing he was holding a small, red
plastic ball.

"Are you *throwing* things at me?"

"I was aiming for the pit," she replied airily. "A few
of the balls spilled out."

He jabbed an index finger in the air to his right.
"The ball pit's *that* way."

"So my aim's a little off."

She made a liar of herself by bending over, grabbing
another plastic sphere off the darkened floor and
winging it at him. Ducking to evade it, Sean honestly
didn't know whether to laugh or grab her to make her
stop and listen to him for a minute.

When she bent to retrieve another one, his feet made
the decision for him. Before she could toss it—
probably aiming for his head this time—he charged her.

"That's enough, darlin'," he muttered, grasping her
upraised hand in his. He backed her against the wall,
until their bodies melded together, all her soft curves
giving way to his hard edges. Palpable anger rolled off
her. It was matched by something else: pure, physical
excitement.

His body responded immediately. His cock, already
half-aroused from the crazy conversation he'd initiated
in her office, swelled and hardened. Unable to resist the
primal urge, he pushed against her, unerringly finding
the warm, soft hollow between her thighs that seemed
designed to welcome him. Even through their clothes

he could tell she was hot and wet, as ready as he was. Groaning, he thrust again, telling her without a doubt how much he wanted her.

"Were you really going to just walk out of here?" she asked, suddenly sounding more aroused than indignant. "With *that* in your pants?"

"It generally goes with me," he said, having to laugh, despite the intensity of the moment.

Annie arched toward him, gasping as she tilted her hips to gain exactly the contact she most needed. "I mean…"

"I know what you mean," he growled, rubbing his face in her soft hair, "I've been trying to give you time, slow this down."

"Slow's overrated."

"I'm beginning to figure that out," he muttered as he closed the distance between their mouths to kiss her. Their tongues mated quickly, wildly, then they both pulled away to gasp for breath.

Realizing he was still clutching her wrist, he let her go, but did not step away, as irresistibly drawn to her as he was to the pull of gravity.

She stared up at him, her eyes glittering in the darkness. Finally, as if unable to hide it any longer, she demanded that he make a decision. *"Well?"*

He didn't have to think for long. "Yes."

Sean could have bundled her out the door, into her van. He could have tried to make it back to her place before letting himself be overwhelmed by his need of her. Would have at least carried her back into her office and slammed the door behind them.

But it was too late. There was no time, no thought, no reason. Only pure, physical response programmed deep in his genetic code that said, *take, have, do.*

Driven by desperate, immediate want, he reached around, picked her up by the waist and carried her a few feet to the huge, colorful ball pit she had *not* been aiming for. Tossing her into it, he followed her down, rolling onto his back and bringing her on top of him.

Their weight pushed him farther into the pit as the balls separated around them, but Sean didn't care. Not giving the time and place another thought, he thrust his hands into Annie's hair, cupped her head and dragged her mouth to his for another hot, hungry kiss.

She was voracious, greedily taking every thrust of his tongue and plunging her own deep into his mouth. Without allowing their lips to part, they both reached for their clothes, Annie clawing his shirt free of his waistband, him unbuttoning her pants and shoving the zipper down.

Slow down, a voice demanded. He knew how to make love to a woman, how to work his way around her body's natural defenses, to drive her crazy with almost-caresses and nearly-there touches until she was a quivering mess in his hands.

But Sean was too far gone for that. Primal lust had taken over his brain. There was no calculating, no planning, no setting a predetermined course and going through familiar motions. Not now. Not with Annie.

There could be no slowing, not when he could hear her desperate whimpers, feel her sweet mouth sucking at his, smell the peachy scent of her skin mixed with the womanly musk of her aroused body.

"Got to feel you," he muttered, reaching under her shirt, dying to touch one of her delicate breasts.

Annie had other ideas. She grabbed his hand and shoved it down, between her legs, telling him exactly where she most wanted him to go.

No slowing down for her, either, it appeared.

Groaning with hunger, he slid his hand through her open zipper. Sean shoved past the thin elastic edge of her panties, tangling his fingers in her curls, wishing he could see but content, for now, to simply touch. She thrust her tongue harder against his when his fingertips brushed against her clit, as if silently telling him to keep going, to never stop.

He'd sooner stop his heart from beating.

He continued to stroke her, tiny flicks, deeper caresses, until she had to pull her mouth away from his to gasp for breath. And when he dipped his hand lower, to part the plump, juicy lips of her sex, she cried out.

"Sweet Annie," he muttered, certain he'd never felt anything so warm and wet. "I can't wait to be *here*." He plunged his finger deep into her channel, feeling all that heat close around him in creamy welcome.

"Sean!" She didn't say anything else. She didn't need to. She just took what he was giving her, as if knowing he was getting as much pleasure from it as she was.

Lord, was the woman tight. Steamy. Every ounce of blood that wasn't already crammed into the veins of his cock raced there in sheer, greedy demand.

When he began to withdraw, Annie thrust against him, demanding more. He gave her another finger, another deep plunge, loving the way mindless pleasure washed over her face.

Knowing how to double that pleasure, he reached farther. Using his long fingers to his advantage, Sean found that spot up inside her that would give her the kind of orgasm many women never experienced.

He knew he'd found it when she stopped moving and gasped.

Then he began stroking her in earnest. He toyed with her, played both spots—inside, as well as outside, with his thumb on her clit—like she was a beautiful little instrument designed to perfectly fit his hand.

And within minutes he was rewarded. Annie flung her head back, rocking hard against his palm, until a climax so strong it made her shake all over ravaged her and she collapsed right onto him.

FOR A FEW LONG, silent moments, Annie lay there on top of Sean, hearing his raging heartbeat, feeling his chest move with his choppy breaths. She tangled her fingers in his loose hair, loving the silky texture of it. Unable to resist, she also toyed with the tiny gold earring, thinking of him as one of those pirate heroes more than ever, considering she'd been picked up and tossed to the nearest surface so he could have his wicked way with her.

Eventually, she began to stir. She'd been satisfied, but only for the moment. Because there was more to do. *So* much more.

But not here. Not only were they a few feet from a huge window that faced the street, but they were also inside a children's play area.

"Thank God we don't let any of the kids who aren't potty-trained in here," she whispered. "And that we have the cleaning crew swap out and sanitize the balls every Saturday."

Sean was silent for a minute, then he groaned and slowly withdrew his hand from her pants. He flexed it, probably because she'd been, sort of, uh, clenching it with her thighs.

"I think I could have lived my whole life without hearing that."

"Sorry. I mean, I'm *not* sorry about what just happened—" *and what was hopefully going to happen next* "—but the place, well…"

"Have a *Murphy* bed hidden in your office?" he asked, sounding so hopeful and pleased with himself at the play on his name that she chuckled slightly.

"No." Smiling with pure wicked anticipation, she added, "My *desk,* however…"

He didn't even wait for her to finish the sentence. Pushing himself up out of the mess of balls, he worked his way out of the pit, then reached for her hand. "Come on."

Annie stared up at him, licking her lips as the glow from the moon caught the gleam in his eyes and turned them into midnight blue jewels glittering in the night. His hair was tangled, his lips parted and his breathing jagged. As if he could barely hold on to his control.

She hadn't managed to get his shirt off, though it was untucked, hanging loosely over his belt. But it wasn't long enough to disguise the large, thick bulge pressing against his zipper.

Oh, how she wanted that.

Tugging her pants back into place, she let him pull her out of the pit. But she didn't straighten all the way up. Instead, she crouched low, intentionally moving her face close to his trousers, letting her breaths wash over him, and her lips brush ever-so-slightly against the bulge.

"I want to see you," she whispered.

He wrapped his hands in her hair.

"Taste you."

The hands tightened.

"Swallow you."

"God in heaven," he groaned.

Finally, knowing she was close to forgetting that damned window again, she rose to her feet. Her fingers laced in his, Annie tugged him with her and hurried back to her office. She'd barely made it through the door when he was on her again, spinning her around and clenching her in his arms. His mouth was ravenous against hers as his tongue plunged deep.

His shirt came off easily between one kiss and the next.

Hers did, too, between one rough caress and the next.

He cupped her face as he pressed a hot kiss on the side of her neck. "It's too dark in here."

Stepping away, she reached for the desk lamp, flipping a switch. Suddenly a warm pool of yellow light banished the blackness and they took the opportunity to devour one another with their eyes.

They stood a foot apart, and for a long moment, neither of them spoke. Annie doubted, however, that the man had been struck dumb at the sight of her, as she'd been by him. Especially because he'd seen just about every single bit of it the night before at her apartment.

She hadn't seen him, though. And he took her breath away. Because she didn't think she'd ever beheld anything more perfectly constructed.

It was no wonder his tux had looked tailor-made, because she didn't imagine any off-the-rack size would ever work on the man. Not with the contrast between those strong, thick-muscled shoulders, that broad chest, the slim waist and his lean hips.

A sparse whorl of dark, crisp hair highlighted the ridges of muscle beneath his skin, and emphasized the flatness of his stomach as it trailed in a thin line down into his pants. And the man didn't have a six-pack, it had to be at least a twelve.

"What on earth are *you* doing with *me?*" she whispered.

He tsked and shook his head, his gaze locked on her body, heat and appreciation shining from his eyes. "You truly have no idea of your own appeal, do you?"

Lifting one strong hand, he touched her cheek, then stared down at her body. "You are incredibly beautiful," he whispered. "So feminine and delicate."

Annie didn't usually feel feminine and delicate. She reserved those descriptions for petite females—which she wasn't. Of average height, she had never been the type of woman men towered over. But her wrist had seemed tiny in his big hand, her waist slender when wrapped in his strong arms.

Her sex small and tight around his thick fingers.

"You are everything a woman should be," he murmured, still staring at her.

Her white bra was lacy and pretty, but certainly didn't produce miraculous curves she simply did not possess. Yet he looked at her as if she was woman incarnate. Like he'd die if he didn't get to touch her, taste her.

He confirmed it by lifting her and depositing her right on top of her desk, spreading her thighs so he could step between them. She spared one moment to be grateful that she was impeccably neat and kept almost nothing on top of the big oak surface, then got right back into the moment, tugged there by the need in his voice.

"I could spend hours telling you how attracted I am to you, how much I want you," he admitted as he kissed his way down her neck, "but I'd rather just *have* you instead."

Annie could only moan when he reached around to unfasten her bra, tugging it off her. The dark appreciation in his eyes spoke volumes, told her all the things he hadn't said.

Yes, his way of communicating was *very* effective. Because judging by that heat, by his ragged breathing, the flexing of muscle in his chest and arms, and that immense ridge in his trousers, he wanted her *desperately*.

He wasn't as wild and unrestrained as he'd been in the other room…but Annie couldn't even think to complain. Not when his mouth felt so good, his lips and tongue tasting a trail across the curve of one breast, then over to the other.

"Please," she whimpered as he continued to avoid her sensitized nipples. They were hard and tilted up toward his mouth in blatant invitation. Yet he didn't give her what she needed, only letting his warm breaths occasionally graze across them.

Annie tightened her legs around his, tugging him closer and sliding against him, up and down, tormenting both of them through their clothes.

"Annie…" he growled.

"Give me what I want and I'll show mercy," she said, dropping her head back until her hair brushed the surface of the desk.

He did, finally covering her nipple and sucking hard. The sensation ignited an invisible power cord inside Annie and she gasped at the power of it. The deliciously ruthless suckling on her breast sent jolt after jolt of pleasure through her body, to land right at the pulsing spot between her legs.

Crying out, she jerked against him, making a liar of herself. Because there was not one ounce of mercy in the wild gyrations of her hips, in the taunting way she rode him. She took mindless pleasure from his rigid cock in the only way she could get it, given their state of dress.

"Annie," he groaned.

She wound her hands in his hair, tugging him up so she could see those incredible eyes. "Take me, Sean. *Now*." Catching his mouth with hers, she thrust her tongue between his lips and set the hard, pulsing rhythm she wanted him to take up inside her.

"You drive me crazy," he muttered, all resistance disappearing as he thrust against her. He reached for his belt and quickly unfastened it. "Insane." The trousers went down to his hips. "Wild." His dark, form-fitting briefs followed. "Mad."

Annie bit her lip when she saw the big, hard ridge of heat that was about to fill her. She'd had well-built lovers, but none had ever instilled such immediate, greedy lust, so that all other thought, all inhibition completely disappeared.

Shaking in anticipation, she couldn't keep her hands steady enough to push her own unfastened pants down. Sean quickly did it for her, tugging them—and her tiny panties—off as she lifted her hips from the surface of the desk.

Annie toed her shoes off and kicked her clothes to the floor, then realized Sean was staring down at her, a predatory smile on his sensual mouth.

"I intend to thoroughly explore that beautiful spot," he said, not taking his eyes off her glistening sex, parted and waiting for him. "Later."

The promise was enough to make her rethink her demands that he take her now. Because a thorough exploration of her most sensitive parts from that incredible mouth, that amazing tongue, suddenly sounded like pure heaven.

Then she caught sight of the erection he was covering with a condom he'd produced from his pants pocket. And she licked her lips, knowing what she most wanted right now.

To be completely filled by him.

She wrapped her bare legs around his lean hips, loving the sensation of his rougher skin, the wiry hair of his legs against her smooth inner thighs. Then she tugged him back where she wanted him.

This time, though, he was the one who showed no mercy. Because instead of plunging into her, he slid his erection against the outside lips of her sex. Riding up and down, he drenched himself with her body's moisture, passing that ridge of heat over her clit until she could hardly breathe.

"Sean!" She arched up, demanding penetration.

He didn't tease her any longer, and she wondered how much effort it had cost him to drag out those intense moments of anticipation.

"I know," he muttered.

Then he thrust hard, burying himself inside her. Annie jerked, so deeply penetrated she instinctively slid back on the desk.

"Yes," she cried, falling completely back to lie flat, lacking the strength to even hold herself up. Every bit of energy she had was focused deep inside her, where this incredible man was imprinting himself with hard, slow thrusts.

But even that didn't seem to be enough for him. Without warning, he grabbed her legs, lifting them. Still too caught up in the incredible sensations, she barely realized what he was doing until he'd pressed a kiss on the inside of her calf. Then he slid it up over his shoulder, quickly following with the other.

"Sean…oh," she whimpered, feeling the extra depth of penetration the position provided. The man was hitting places in her body she didn't know existed.

And she absolutely loved it.

"Are you all right?" he asked, pausing to make sure she was still with him.

She was. Barely. Most of her had floated away to pleasure island to savor the delicious assault on every one of her nerve endings. "Most definitely."

"Good." He didn't add them but she heard the words *because I'm not stopping* anyway.

Sean's need took over. He was slick with sweat, his muscles flexing as he took them both higher. He'd drive hard for a few incredible strokes, then slow his pace, kissing her calf, running the tip of his fingers down the back of her leg. Until she'd twist beneath him, wanting it hard and fast again.

The pleasure was intense, unreal. But it wasn't taking her *exactly* where she needed to go. And as if he knew that, Sean paused, his cock still buried to the hilt inside her, and dropped his hand to her inner thigh.

"Come for me, Annie," he whispered, then he stroked her clit with his thumb.

She came instantly. As if her body had simply been waiting for his husky, erotic invitation. Screaming slightly, she rode it out, every muscle she had reflexively tightening, then relaxing.

And before she'd even recovered from it, Sean resumed his thrusts, until, within moments, he threw his head back, groaned, and climaxed inside her.

ANNIE INSISTED on driving him back to his hotel. Despite his protests that he could catch a cab, she refused to be dissuaded.

That was how Sean had found himself sitting inside an American-made minivan that had stuffed toys on the backseat, a pair of baby Nikes dangling from the rearview mirror, and a magnetic door sign proclaiming to the world that he was riding in a kid-mobile. It wasn't his usual mode of conveyance. But he didn't really give a damn.

"I wish you'd come up with me," he murmured as Annie pulled up outside his hotel. A doorman eyed them dubiously, but Sean waved him off when he began to walk over to open the door. "Take a nice, hot bath, let me massage any muscles that might be a little…sore?"

Annie nibbled on her bottom lip, still swollen from his kisses. He imagined her throat was probably dry and scratchy from all the moaning and screaming she'd been doing, too. He tried to tempt her further. "I can order a bottle of champagne from room service to soothe your throat, help you relax."

"You're very tempting."

He was a professional, he damn well should be. Not that he was ready to tell her that. Not now. And considering he honestly didn't think he was ever even going to see her again after this weekend, probably not ever.

He tried to shove away the dismay that came with the mental acknowledgement that theirs was only a one-weekend affair. *That's all you have room for*, a voice reminded him. *All you've ever wanted.*

Or all he'd ever wanted…before now. But he couldn't dwell on that, not yet, not until he had a moment to analyze just what these feelings he was experiencing for Annie really were.

"So you'll…come?" He caressed the final word,

knowing that now, with the first heated, intense coupling over with, he'd have the strength to slow down and pleasure her until she was drowning in orgasms.

She put the vehicle into Park and turned in her seat to look at him. "You'll seduce me."

"Undoubtedly."

"I'll end up staying the whole night."

"God, I hope so."

She sighed, as if regretting what she was about to say. Which meant *he* was going to regret it.

"Sean, I can barely bring my thighs together as it is. If I spend a whole night with you, all weekend I'm going to walk like a woman who's been *done* to within an inch of her life."

The most masculine part of him couldn't prevent a self-satisfied chuckle at her frank revelation.

She didn't seem to notice. "This weekend's going to be hard enough without me looking so obviously…"

"Satisfied?"

"*Gluttonous.* Like someone who's gorged herself on something rich and fattening until she can't even move."

"That I'd like to see. How much would be too much, do you think?"

Her glare told him she didn't appreciate him making light of the situation. "We have to leave early in the morning if we're going to make lunch, which I promised we would. So I need to go…"

"Take a hot bubble bath and drink a glass of champagne?" he asked, sounding as innocent as he could.

She thrust a little punch at his upper arm, poking him with a bony knuckle. "Shut up."

"Shutting."

"And get out."

"I must admit, I'm startin' to feel a wee bit used."

Her gasp told him she'd fallen for that, but her subsequent frown told him it hadn't been for long. "Like any single man alive wouldn't want to be *used* like that."

"Well, now, I didn't say I didn't like it."

She flipped a button to unlock all the doors in the van. Probably some protective device to make sure no little heathens tumbled out of the car in the middle of the street. "Go."

Knowing there was no changing her mind, he reached for the door handle. "Fine, fine." Then, certain he wouldn't possibly last throughout the next forty-eight hours without tasting her again, he leaned over and slid his hand into her hair. Pressing a soft kiss on her mouth, he breathed her in, soaked her up, feeling her body relax as she parted her lips in welcome.

A beeping horn intruded, and Sean ended the kiss. "See you in the morning," he said.

She smiled gently. "Early."

"Right."

"Sean?" she asked, her tone husky, her lips moist. "I wish I could stay."

Hearing the genuine regret, he could only echo it. "So do I. Goodnight, Annie." He opened the door and stepped out. "By the way, be prepared to park this charming vehicle here tomorrow morning. I'll be driving."

He would have offered to pick her up at her place, but honestly, Sean was thinking ahead. He liked the idea of her coming back here to the hotel with him late Sunday afternoon…all the better to tempt her to spend the entire night in it.

"I didn't think you had a car!"

"I don't," he replied with a cocky grin. "But it's covered, anyway."

"I can't show up at my folks' place in a limo."

"Not a chance," he said. "You think I want them to immediately take me for either a spoiled rich punk, a pimp or a drug dealer?"

She laughed and rolled her eyes. "As if."

"Seriously, don't worry about it. The hotel has a car rental service. I've got it covered."

That was true. The hotel had a *luxury* car rental service that was exorbitantly expensive, but would be well worth it. First, it would enable him to avoid another ride in a pram disguised as a full-fledged vehicle. And *he* could drive, letting Annie relax for the long ride to her folks, when he knew she'd already be feeling worked up and worried.

"Fine," she said, accepting his explanation without further questions. Probably because she wanted to go— to get out of here, now, before he tried again to tempt her to stay.

He could. Part of him wanted to.

Another part—the part that saw the fatigue around her eyes and the way she kept shifting in the driver's seat, as if she truly was a little uncomfortable—knew better.

She had a stressful couple of days ahead of her. Best that she go into it refreshed after a good, uninterrupted night of sleep. Not physically uncomfortable after a good, wild night of lovemaking.

But when they got back here on Sunday, after he helped her pull off her little charade in front of her family? Well, then, all bets were off.

He'd take what he wanted. Give her what she hadn't asked for. Then he'd be able to say goodbye to her knowing they'd both gotten more than they'd ever dreamed of out of her single bid at the auction.

7

ANNIE HAD SEEN SLEEK, ridiculously expensive convertibles like the one Sean had rented, but she'd never actually ridden in one. So she'd never heard the way the engine's powerful roar actually sounded more like a smooth rumble from the inside. Nor had she realized the engine's power felt tangible, like the vehicle was a living creature harnessed and impatient to *go*.

"God, this car is sexy," she said, amazed at how good it felt to just ride, watching the miles slip past as the car's broad tires skimmed over the steaming blacktop below.

"Handles beautifully, too," he said, talking loud enough to be heard over the wind and the music. "Maybe you can get behind the wheel for a while later."

Not a chance. With her luck, she'd drive it into a ravine and end up having to sell a kidney to pay for the damage.

"That's okay, I'm fine here," she said, settling deeper into the buttery-soft leather seat.

Usually the two-and-a-half-hour trip back home seemed interminable and boring. Each mile passing under her *minivan's* plodding tires always darkened her mood.

Though she adored her family and loved going home for holidays, there was always the inevitable conversation she'd give anything to avoid. The one where they all cornered her and demanded that she at last admit she was lonely and miserable living away from them all in the big city.

That she never did—and that it wasn't true—didn't keep them from repeating the refrain during at least one family meeting every single time.

This trip, though, was shaping up to be entirely different. Maybe it was the man by her side, whose presence would provide some physical barrier and also, hopefully, get the clan off her back for a little while. Or hell, maybe it was just the sheer pleasure of riding under the brilliant, bright blue sky, with the wind blowing wildly in her hair and hard rock music pouring from the speakers.

It was…freeing. That was a good word for it. She felt free of her family expectations, her business stresses, her ugly romantic history.

Free to just enjoy the wind in her face and the strong, solid presence of the man sitting beside her. And while she would very much like to feel free enough to ask that man to pull over and make love to her under the vivid summer sky, she knew they didn't have the time. Not for the kind of lovemaking she wanted to do with him now.

Last night had been hard and fast and frantic. Utterly mind-blowing.

Today? If she had her way and could actually get him to pull over into a secluded country lane? She'd want hours and hours of deep, sensual pleasure under the hot, drugging rays of the sun.

Annie shifted in her seat, still tender. She was very aware of his possession of last night, and wanted so much more she could barely stand the wait.

"Thank you for driving," she said, needing to think about something else. She spoke loudly to be heard over the engine, the music and the wind. "Though, I think this car is expensive enough to put those pimp or drug dealer thoughts into a normal person's mind."

"We'll make sure they know it's a rental."

As if he knew she had been thanking him for even more, Sean reached over and put his hand on hers, squeezing lightly. "It would be nice to just keep on heading west until we hit the Pacific." He wagged his eyebrows. "Or to pull over and have a nice, long…picnic." Shaking his head, he added, "But we are almost there."

How, she wondered, could the man be so intuitive, knowing that she'd love nothing more than to keep on going, see something new—*the big beautiful ocean*—and skip the whole ordeal with her folks altogether? Why did he seem to know her so well after a few short days when her own family hardly knew her at all after twenty-seven years?

Had anyone? Really, had there ever been a single person who'd totally gotten her? Not just her goals, but her deepest dreams, her conflicts, the way she was torn between wanting to seek out new experiences and yet also have the warmth and happiness of family? The daring to see the world…and the stability of a home and a life filled with love and warmth?

She didn't think so. Not ever.

Sean released her hand, needing to downshift, and distracted her from her morose thoughts. "How's the big boy holding up back there?"

She glanced at the backseat. Wally, who was usually very fussy in the van, had settled in nicely. He was sprawled in his crate, either asleep or doing a good impression of being that way. Though sheltered from most of the wind, he obviously enjoyed the feel of it ruffling his belly fur because he appeared completely comfortable.

She still couldn't get over how the ultraspoiled cat had taken to Sean right away. Wally obviously liked the man's touch as much as Annie did.

Don't even go there, she reminded herself. Riding beside Sean, feeling his heat, smelling that musky, male scent of his skin, was distracting enough. Giving in to the memories of every delicious moment the night before would probably have her saying to hell with the time, and demanding that he pull over.

As they passed a sign stating the exit for Green Springs was only ten miles ahead, Sean reached to flip off the powerful stereo. "I think maybe I could use a primer."

"What?"

"We covered so many details last night…maybe you should test me. Though, of course, there's no question that I remember what you wear to bed." Then, a self-satisfied tone in his voice, added, "Or that I now know exactly where your *real* ticklish spot is."

Oh, boy. Annie shifted in the seat, suddenly a lot hotter than she'd been a moment before under the direct rays of the sun.

"But I don't suppose anybody will be asking about those things."

"Definitely not." Glad for the chance to focus on their arrival, not how much she wanted Sean to stop and do all the things to her that he hadn't done last night, she thought about the most crucial issues. The things a man who'd been dating her for a few months would absolutely know about.

"What are my brothers' names?"

"Jed's the oldest, and he's engaged to Becca. Then Steve, who's one year older than you and is the ladies' man of the family." He rattled the details off rapidly, obviously a quick study. "Randy is the baby, and he's interested in joining the Air Force, though he hasn't yet worked up a set of ballocks as big as yours to tell your parents that."

She snorted, taking that as a compliment. "Right. But don't say a word."

"Wouldn't dream of it." He narrowed his eyes in concentration. "Hmm…what else…oh, Randy's almost twenty-one. That's easy to remember, since my sister's the same age."

That was the first time he'd mentioned a family member other than his parents, and the affectionate smile hinted at a close relationship. "Sister? Where is she?"

"Back in Ireland."

"Do you get to see her often?"

"Almost never. Moira and I mostly keep in touch by phone and e-mail." He was silent for a moment, then, as if he'd weighed his options and decided he could trust her with more of himself, he continued. "I had a falling out with my father several years ago and haven't been back home since."

"I see."

"No, you probably don't," he muttered. "I can hear in your voice when you talk about them that you adore your family, even though they drive you 'round the bend."

"When I don't want to shove them all in a river."

He chuckled. "Still, there's genuine affection there."

"But none in yours?"

He pushed his silky black hair off his face—the wind had tugged it free of its ponytail. Oh, Lord, was her father going to have something to say about that, and the tiny gold earring flashing from one lobe. "I love my father," he admitted, sounding as though it hurt him to say it out loud. "But affection comes with a price in my family. If you pay it, all's well and good. If you don't…"

"Then you have to keep in touch with your sister only by phone and e-mail."

"That's about it. Although whenever she has a class trip off the island, I try to arrange a business trip to meet up with her." A wicked laugh escaped his lips. "I showed her the hot spots in Prague when she was seventeen and the strip in Amsterdam a year later."

Annie snorted, able to picture it. "Intentionally trying to corrupt her?"

"Just trying to let her live a little, since our father and her mother have clamped down on her pretty hard because of the choices I've made."

"That's a shame."

Although he didn't frown or otherwise appear to regret telling her as much as he had, he immediately returned to the subject at hand. "Is your relationship with your brothers anything like that?"

"My brothers couldn't find Prague on a map," she muttered, then sighed at her own tone. "Sorry. That was bitchy. They're very nice guys. Steve and I were like twins when we were kids. Practically inseparable."

"But?"

"But," she explained with a simple shrug of her shoulders, "they never left home. Never wanted to. Never will. Randy wants to join the service because he's young and patriotic…but if he does it, he'll still come back here afterward to live out the rest of his days."

"While you couldn't wait to go live out yours almost anywhere else."

"Exactly. I had posters of foreign cities on the walls of my room growing up, maps, brochures from the Peace Corps, even the military. Anything that would take me someplace far away and different."

His eyebrows shot up and he turned to cast a quick, surprised glance at her. "The Peace Corps? Yes. But the military?" Shaking his head at the very possibility, he didn't even have to say what he was thinking.

Not that he was wrong. "Hey, I was just thinking of all the angles." Remembering the brouhaha that had accompanied the arrival of an envelope from the Army with her name on it during high school, she rolled her eyes. "But I didn't seriously pursue it. My father told me he'd lock me in the basement if I even thought about enlisting."

He chuckled.

"My mother was worse. She told me I'd be putting my brothers' lives at risk because all of *them* would have to enlist, too, to keep me safe, including Randy, who was eleven at the time."

Damn, her mother was good at getting her own way. At least, she *had* been. Not anymore. Annie had had her taste of freedom and she'd never give it up. "That's another reason he's delaying telling them he wants to sign up now," she added.

"Twenty-one's better than eleven," he said with a laugh. The laughter quickly faded and his tone became serious. "Chicago's not far enough for you, though, is it? Not in the long run."

Funny that he'd figured that out so quickly. "I love Chicago, and I'm not at all unhappy there. I've got a great business and lots of friends, and someday I'm sure I'll be happy to settle down and raise a family there."

"But?"

"*But* you can bet I'm hoarding my pennies so that I can see some of the world before that day comes." She shook her head and stared at the trees whipping by along the side of the highway. "To the rest of the Davises, Green Springs *is* the world, and that's exactly the way they like it."

"Different dreams," he mused, his voice so low, she almost didn't hear it over the wind. "None better. None worse. Just different."

Different dreams. That's what it all came down to.

She didn't reply, didn't need to. Because with those words, he'd nailed it. Why Annie had left, why her family had been upset about it. Why she hated going back to deal with their disappointment again and again. Even why Sean was sitting beside her in the car, about to help her get through the weekend with a combination of half-truths and excuses.

She had different dreams…which they didn't understand.

Yet somehow, the man sitting beside her, who she'd known for less than a week, did.

SEAN DIDN'T QUITE know what he was expecting when he pulled up the narrow lane to Annie's childhood home. He'd certainly seen plenty of farms back in Ireland, many of them on Murphy land his father had rented out to others. But most of those were small, family-run operations with sheep grazing on lush green fields, a dash of color on their backs distinguishing one owner's flock from the next. Small cottages would dot the landscape, with ramshackle barns and old-fashioned plows rusting in the fields.

Nothing like this.

"Good God, it looks like a factory!" he said as he

drove alongside the enormous, entirely modern barn, two stories tall, and a few hundred feet long.

A small fleet of trucks was parked at the end of it, all bearing the same dairy logo of a jolly cow. Impeccably maintained equipment was visible through the wide-open doors of another building, and several workers dressed in khakis and uniform shirts were in sight.

"I was picturing something more like…"

"Green Acres?"

He glanced at Annie, who had noted his surprise and was amused by it. "What's that?"

"An ancient show on *TVLand* about…never mind, it doesn't matter." She pointed to the top of a hill beyond the barns and a huge, sloping field where horses grazed lazily under the bright June sky. "There's the house."

Another surprise.

Annie's parents' home was enormous, a sprawling, three-story farmhouse, painted a bright yellow with contrasting white shutters around every window. Curved flower beds overflowing with daffodils that reminded him of home surrounded the broad front porch. Tall shade trees lined the soft green perimeter of a well-tended lawn, which was separated from the pasture by a long picket fence. And a gazebo complete with two-person swing perched at the very edge of a sloping hill that melded into the expansive countryside.

The Davis home was absolutely nothing like he'd pictured.

Shocked into silence because of his own faulty preconceptions, he drove up the hill. Given how wrong he was about the house, he had to wonder if he'd entirely underestimated the family he was about to meet, too.

A hint of misgiving crawled up his spine. Maybe this wasn't going to be the piece of cake he'd figured it for.

Parking on the side of the house between two monstrous trucks and an SUV the size of a building, he heard Annie sigh in audible resignation. "What's wrong?"

"They're all already here," she said, staring at the vehicles.

"Your brothers?"

"Uh-huh. I'd hoped to introduce you slowly, rather than to everybody all at once."

"I thought they all *lived* here."

"Randy does. But Steve and Jed both live in their own houses that they built nearby."

Sean had a sudden suspicion. "On your father's land?"

"He gave them each a hundred acres to build on when they turned twenty-five."

He was starting to get the picture.

"Where's your hundred?" he murmured, watching for her reaction, suspecting what it would be.

He wasn't disappointed. She rubbed a hand over her eyes, sighed, then waved a hand generally toward the east.

"I see."

Not only was he getting the picture, he'd begun to realize just how *big* that picture was. Annie was in no way the simple small-town girl she'd made herself out to be. Her family had to be rich as Croesus, running a highly successful dairy farm, owning the land as far as he could see. Which could explain their overprotectiveness toward Annie.

Sean hadn't worried *too* much about meeting them, given his "crash course" and his ability to get along with just about anyone. Oh, he'd been prepared for them not to like him because of how much they wanted Annie to come home, but that was a natural thing, not too much of a concern.

Now that he saw the way they lived, however, he began to understand why, and to anticipate the true depth of their imminent dislike.

She was the only daughter in a wealthy, close-knit family who built their homes within miles of each other to make sure everyone stayed together. While Sean was the only son in a wealthy family who still tried to arrange marriages, for God's sake.

He wondered what she'd say if she knew just how similar their backgrounds were. That he understood her a lot more than she might imagine.

He also wondered if it was a good thing, or a bad one, that his heart twisted in his chest for her when he realized how serious she'd been about her difficult family life.

He'd come here thinking her a typical I-can't-go-home-without-a-man single girl. But she'd *meant* it. Her situation was every bit as tough as his own.

She'd chosen to escape by taking care of small children. He'd done so by taking care of the needs of strange women. Different…but rooted in the same dream of independence from the expectations of family.

He and Annie had the same dreams.

Sean was almost stunned by the depth of understanding—emotion—he suddenly felt toward the beautiful, strong-willed woman sitting beside him. The lengths she'd gone to might not have been as extreme as his, but she'd fought hard to get where she was, and to stay there. Including paying out a large sum of money that he suspected she couldn't afford—since she didn't live like her family supported her—to maintain her independence.

By bidding on *him*.

He'd do anything he could to help her. Anything except confide in her. Because Sean wasn't anywhere near ready to tell her just how well he understood her plight, and what a similar kind of desperation had driven *him* to do.

He'd never much cared about his lifestyle, or what anyone thought of it, with the exception of his sister. And now…now, he realized with a sinking heart, Annie.

Shit. He was in trouble here. Wanting to get away, fast. Wanting more to pull her into his arms and tell her he understood, that she wasn't alone.

But, damn it, *he was*. Alone. Always. And that's the way his life had to stay.

Wasn't it?

"I think this place is bigger than my family's estate," he finally muttered, staring out the windshield at the sweeping landscape below. The vibrant green hillside and valley below it were dotted with a few sheep…he'd been waiting for those fluffy buggers.

"Estate?" She chuckled, distracted from her melancholy. "Are you a pampered little rich boy?"

"Not pampered," he clarified as he turned to see her watching him. He took no offense at her laughter. Not when she was finally relaxed, smiling, at least a bit, her eyes reflecting back the soft blue of the sky overhead.

"Should I call you *Lord* Murphy?"

Wouldn't his father love that. "Nope. One of my drunkard ancestors lost the title—and half his land—by ticking off some royal or another a million years ago."

Her jaw dropped open. She'd been joking. He hadn't.

"Oh, wow," she finally said, sounding stunned. "I guess I should have gotten a complete primer on *you*."

That wasn't going to happen. Not if Sean could help it.

Though, he supposed a few minor details would be smart. Especially since he'd realized this weekend might not be as easy as he'd originally thought. Not if this wealthy, small-town family had *millions* of reasons to be overprotective of their only girl.

"I drink tea, not coffee. Sweet, no cream," he admitted, trying to think of what might possibly come up during the brief visit. "Dark beer only—light is for infants. Murphy's is best, but you can never find it on tap on this continent." Racking his brain, he added, "I went to Trinity College in Dublin, have been known to knock men unconscious on the rugby field…and I speak six languages."

Her eyes widened in shock. *"Six?"*

He shrugged. "I've the Irish gift of the gab." Speaking fast since they could be interrupted at any moment, he continued. "I never stay in one place for long and I have apartments in a couple of cities but not what you'd call a real home in any of them."

"Sad," she murmured.

Maybe to her. To Sean it was the only way he'd ever wanted to live. But he didn't want to explain that—not now, when they had no time. And when he hadn't yet figured out just how much he wanted Annie to know about his life.

Or how much he might be willing to change that life if he could keep her in it for just a little while longer.

Shaking off that unbelievable thought, he went back to what he was good at. Innuendo.

He smiled wickedly, letting her see the heat in his eyes. "One more important detail you should probably know—I don't wear anything to bed."

It worked. Annie licked her lips and raked a hungry stare over his body. The woman looked as predatory as her cat, and Sean would give just about anything to get out of here and let her devour him the way she appeared to want to. "I can't wait to see you in your pajamas then," she whispered.

"Naughty girl. What would the family say?"

Her unconcerned shrug answered that question as she leaned a little closer to whisper, "How many hours do we have to be here again?"

His head filling with all the things he still wanted to do with this woman, he called himself ten kinds of idiot. They'd been friendly and casual all the way down here in the car. Why, now when they were parked right outside her parents' door, did he have to go and provoke her into reminding him of how much he wanted her? Especially given the fact that he was still reeling over the depth of connection he'd discovered between them, and the emotions that discovery had inspired.

As if she, too, suddenly regretted the bad timing, Annie cleared her throat and waved her hand in the air, dismissing the entire subject. "Forget I asked that. It's not like I haven't been counting down the hours since the moment we left your hotel, anyway."

Him, too.

"Let's take up this conversation when we get back in this car for the return trip, okay?"

"Deal."

"Maybe," she said, licking her lips, "we can explore a few backcountry roads tomorrow before we hit the highway."

"Private ones?"

"Oh, most definitely."

Mmm. Car sex under the hot sun. Sounded just about perfect. "I'll hold you to that."

"I'd expect nothing else." Her light mood returning, she asked, "So, is there anything else I should know before I introduce you to the Davis clan? I mean, you aren't, like, tenth in line for the throne of England, right?"

Rolling his eyes, Sean reached over and slid his hand into her silky blond hair, wanting to touch her once more before they had to go in. "You Americans. Don't you know anything about anybody's history but your own?"

"I suppose not," she admitted. Then she turned her face and kissed his palm, her lips soft and moist against his hot skin. "But you're half-American, too, right?"

He nodded, conceding the point, not about to continue teasing her, not when her soft mouth was so gently caressing him, teasing him, driving him wild. Unable to resist more, he pulled his hand away, leaned over—eliminating the slight space left between them—and brushed his mouth against hers. Annie tilted her head to welcome him, her hair, tangled from the ride, falling over his bare forearm.

Kissing her in the sunshine was a new pleasure, bringing with it new, unexpected sensations. The lazy mating of their tongues brought to mind long, lethargic afternoons of slow-and-easy lovemaking that went on for hours. The kind where the object wasn't the final orgasmic destination, but rather the delicious pleasures of the ride.

He probably could have kissed her all day, caressed her soft cheek, inhaled the irresistible peach scent that seemed to cloak her entire body. But suddenly something rapped him on the head and he jerked away.

Fully expecting to see one of her angry brothers, he was shocked to instead find himself face-to-face with a…a… "Good, God, what *is* that thing?"

His eyes wide, he could only stare as an enormous bird leaned into the open convertible again. This time, however, the creature didn't aim his pointy, rock-hard beak at Sean's head, but rather toward Annie's outstretched hand.

"That's Radar." Smiling in visible delight, she rose to her knees on the car's seat, watching as the beast gave an ungainly leap, landed on the hood of the car, then bounced down to stand on the other side of it.

Sean's jaw dropped. There were bird prints on the Ferrari.

Bird prints.

That was going to be interesting to explain to the rental company. Jaysus, considering the size of the beast, he ought to check and make sure there weren't dents beneath the prints.

"Hello, boy, you've missed me, haven't you?" Annie asked as she reached up to tenderly scratch the puff of fluffy feathers on Big Bird's crown.

"What exactly *is* he?" Sean asked, finally tearing his attention away from the circular smears of dirt on the bright red hood.

"An emu."

An emu had just poked him in the head. This didn't bode well for the upcoming weekend.

Behind them, Wally had finally awakened and had caught sight of the newcomer. The big old tabby was on all fours, his back arched, hissing through the top of his cage. Every piece of his fur stood completely on end so that he looked two inches larger all the way around.

"Wally thinks he's fried chicken waiting to happen," Sean said, still shaking his head. "Is there any particular reason your emu friend just poked me?"

"He's a little overprotective," she replied, almost cuddling the overgrown fluff ball, who was now nosing around her silky, sleeveless shirt, as if looking for pockets that might contain food.

When Annie had arrived at the hotel this morning, Sean had studied that shirt. His mouth had gone wet with hunger at the memory of those beautiful, delicate breasts so perfectly highlighted by the fabric.

So he could have told the bird there were no pockets. Because he'd looked. Hard.

"Emus aren't usually terribly friendly. But I raised Radar from infancy. He was my senior 4H project, and he loves me. Now he's just like the family dog, roaming around the yard."

God, Sean wouldn't want to step in anything the beast left lying on the lawn.

"He really is a pussy cat, most of the time. He just doesn't like strangers. He'll have to get used to you."

"I'm sure he does a great job scaring off intruders." If Sean came face-to-face with *that* thing on a dark night, he'd think twice about trying to cross it. Especially if he wanted to wake up the next morning without any new holes in his skull.

Suddenly, as if on cue, that skull was whomped again. "Ow! What the blazes?"

He swung his head around to glare at what *had* to be one of her brothers this time, but instead found another completely unrecognizable creature. "Bloody hell!"

"Bleat," the thing replied, sounding like a wee lamb rather than the drooly, miniature wooly mammoth it most resembled. Despite his travels 'round the world, he'd never seen such an animal in his life.

"Rex!" Annie cried, again sounding delighted.

The beast looked up at the sound of her voice, forgetting Sean's head and the invisible sign that said "Whack me" which he suspected was overtop it. Praying to God the monster didn't leap like the bird had, Sean pointed a finger and gave it a stern glance. "Don't you even *think* about it, fluffy."

"He's an alpaca. Isn't he sweet?"

Appearing girlishly delighted, Annie actually rose to stand on her seat. Bracing herself by putting one hand on the top of the windshield, she bent at the waist and leaned all the way over Sean, toward the driver's side of the car, so she could pet the newcomer.

Sean didn't mind this intrusion so much. Because it put Annie's hip about two inches from his mouth. Her beautiful, slender legs were displayed to incredible advantage beneath the loose, silky skirt she wore. It had fallen forward to reveal the backs of her thighs almost all the way up to her pert bottom. And about two inches of creamy skin was revealed where her shirt pulled free of her waistband.

Starving man, meet all-you-can-eat buffet.

Unable to resist, he slid a hand up the back of one limb, slowly, savoring the texture and the warmth of her, until he was able to caress her inner thigh. It was smooth and supple, incredibly soft. Sean breathed deeply, remembering the way those legs had felt wrapped around his hips last night when he'd been driving into her tight little body.

The memory sent a surge of interest straight into his

lap. Sean actually had to shift in his seat as his cock informed him it was raring to go.

Were they somewhere more private, he'd love nothing more than turning her around to face him. He'd lean her back against the windshield, spreading her legs wide for his intimate perusal. Her beautiful, glistening sex would beckon for his kiss and he'd explore every inch of her in ways he hadn't been able to last night in the frenzy of their first time.

"Your skirt might just as well be red," he muttered, leaning close so his every breath was filled with the scent of her skin. "I'm feeling much like a bull being tempted into charging."

She glanced down at him, apparently only now realizing how tempting her position was to him. "Just call me Matador."

"I'd rather call you naked woman I'll be making love to in two minutes." He glanced up at her and frowned. "Though I guess I'll have to wait and call you that in a little over twenty-four hours."

Not that he could wait that long for at least a sample. Leaning up, he pressed his mouth to that delicious strip of skin at her waist, licking it lightly.

"Mmm," she moaned, closing her eyes, remaining frozen where she was.

"Mmm, indeed," he replied, kissing her again, this time lightly biting the tender flesh just above her hip bone.

Thump.

"Jaysus," he snapped, wondering if Doctor Fecking Dolittle's entire menagerie had decided to attack him.

But it wasn't another furry or feathery creature who stood behind Rex. In fact, this one had skin. More than six feet of it, he'd judge.

He also had blond hair the color of Annie's. And stormy blue eyes. Not to mention a very deep frown.

Brilliant. His hand was up Annie's skirt, her hip was reddened from the sexy nip he'd just taken there.

And he was staring up at one of her overprotective brothers.

8

THIS WASN'T STARTING off very well.

Annie hadn't even heard the approach of her oldest brother, Jed. But she'd heard Sean's surprised grunt, which tore her attention off the pure pleasure she'd been experiencing from his touch. Under the hot sun and the blue sky, with his hand on her thigh and his mouth on her hip, she'd been able to forget for a moment that they were about to go hand-in-hand into the lion's den.

Until one of the stalking beasts had come out of that den and pounced, catching them completely unawares.

"Dad's right on the porch," her brother snapped.

Annie glanced toward the house, but couldn't see it. Sean had parked the tiny sports car between two of the monster trucks her brothers drove, and it was completely hidden from view of the house.

"*Thanks* for coming to get us," she said, making no effort to disguise her sarcasm.

"You were taking so long, he was about to come down and see if you needed help with your luggage."

Right. As if they had a trunk full for an overnight visit. If she knew her father, he'd been counting the seconds on his watch, calculating how long it would take for her and her new guy to reach the porch without any funny stuff going on. That was pretty much how he'd waited for Annie after any date she'd had growing up.

"I was just introducing Rex to Se…" Annie caught herself, but suddenly found it impossible to force the name of someone she loathed onto someone she was beginning to greatly care about. So she quickly amended, "To my friend."

"Rex. Is that what you're calling your butt now?"

She flipped up her middle finger, as she'd often done as a teenager, when their parents were within earshot but not in direct sight-range. "I dunno, is that what you were calling Becca's when I caught you two naked under the tree last Christmas Eve?"

He deflected the counterattack. "She's my fiancée."

"She wasn't *then*." Grinning in pure evil, she added, "And I don't know what *you* were calling *her,* but from what I heard, she thinks you're some kind of deity. '*Oh, God,* yes!'"

Jed barked a quick laugh, dropping the ridiculous protective older brother attitude. His innate good humor appeared in his eyes. "Mom should never have let you watch *Beverly Hills 90210* when you were a kid."

"Oh, right, that explains it. Now move so I can get out."

He moved, stepping away from the car door, opening it, and offering her his hand. Being careful not to kick Sean, or knee him in the head as she stepped over him, she hopped down and threw her arms around her brother's neck. "Missed me?"

"Not that mouth, I haven't," he said. Squeezing her tightly, he added, "But, yeah, I guess we miss the rest of you a little bit."

Then, the typical sibling banter out of the way, he released her and gave his full attention to Sean. And the jaw stiffened. Seeing what *he* was seeing, she suspected she knew why.

Sean was not only so handsome he made other men uncomfortable, but he certainly looked the part of a rebel compared to most of the guys around here. His long hair was loose and windblown, tangled at his nape. His earring flashed gold under the glint of the sun. His dark sunglasses, which he'd shoved up onto his head when they'd arrived, had a designer name that no normal person could afford. And he was driving the kind of car usually reserved for partying movie-star types.

In short, he was everything her brothers would be suspicious of…and everything Annie already knew she adored.

"You must be Jed," Sean said, unfolding his long, lean body as he stepped out of the car. He extended his hand. "She's forgotten to introduce me. The name's Murphy, but everybody calls me Murph."

Gaping, she caught his eye and mouthed, *"Murph?"* garnering a shrug in response.

He was *so* not a Murph. But Sean was obviously doing whatever he could to avoid any confusion about his fake name this weekend. She could kiss him for that.

Well, for a lot of reasons.

Jed shook Sean's hand, and they did that squeeze-the-hand-tightly-to-prove-who's-manlier thing. So stupid, though she suspected Jed was the one trying to prove something. Sean wasn't the type to bother.

Tiring of the let's-compare-balls game, Annie pushed right between the two of them, bending over to reach into the back of the car for Wally's crate.

"Let me do that, darlin'."

"Oh, God, you brought the beast?" Jed asked,

sounding dismayed. Heaven knew why. It's not like the shoes Wally had christened for him had been Italian, and he most certainly stepped in worse here on the farm. So Wally had piddled in his boots once. Or twice….

"What was I supposed to do, leave him home alone to be miserable and starve?"

"He could have pounced on a burglar if he got hungry," Jed said, eyeing the cat warily.

Instead of just grabbing the crate, as Annie had intended to do, Sean actually opened the top of it, reaching in to scoop Wally out. The animal should have been skittish and aggressive after being cooped up for a couple of hours. In the past, he'd even bitten Annie once or twice after a long road trip.

Instead, Wally curled against Sean's chest and tucked his head beneath his chin, delicately licking his paw and glaring at her older brother.

Jed gawked.

And Annie suppressed a grin. The mere fact that Sean had won over Wally should send a signal about her new "boyfriend" and just how much a part of Annie's life he was.

Even if he wasn't. Not for long, at least.

Don't think that way, she reminded herself as a sharp stab of something like disappointment thrust into her belly. She had at least another day and a half with the man. And she needed to make the most of it. Because it was *all* she'd ever have with him.

He'd made that clear. She'd accepted the terms. End of story.

Till tomorrow night only.

Oh, did she wish they didn't have to spend the bulk of that remaining time here.

"Come on, before he sends down reinforcements," Jed said as he turned toward the house. Her brother was so stunned by Sean's friendship with Wally that he forgot to be a belligerent asshole about seeing Sean's hand stuck up Annie's skirt. Instead, he silently led them up the driveway toward the porch, where the other Davis men stood at attention.

"Good grief," she muttered. "Why didn't you all just dig out the shotguns and start picking the chew out of your teeth with hunting knives?"

Beside her, Sean snorted a laugh, but Jed just kept walking. "Here they are," he called. "Annie had to stop and say hello to her furry and feathered friends before greeting her own family."

Huh. No mention of Sean's mouth on her hip. That wasn't too surprising. Jed might be a bossy big brother, but he was not a loudmouth.

Then again, he was probably keeping his mouth shut for his own benefit. He knew Annie well enough to expect serious payback if he made a fuss.

No way would he want her to spill the beans about the Christmas Eve rendezvous, which had taken place right beside their mother's beloved antique nativity set. Baby Jesus and all the angels and shepherds must have gotten quite an eyeful. As had Annie, who'd crept downstairs for a late-night sneak peek at the presents after everyone had *supposedly* gone to bed. Instead, she'd gotten the kind of peek no woman *ever* wanted to get of her own brother's backside.

Eww.

"Here's our girl!" Her father came down from the porch, followed by her brothers, and they all encircled her for big, boisterous hugs meant to remind her that she was the little woman and they big, strong men.

She was passed around the group for more macho embracing. If one of them squeezed too hard and picked her up until her toes dragged the ground again, she was going to puke right over his shoulder.

God, was she glad Sean was no he-man.

"Well, are you going to introduce us?" her father asked, his chin up as he gave Sean a once-over.

Sean had been a darling asking Jed to call him Murph, but there was no way Annie could say it all weekend without laughing. Sounded too much like Smurf. And a cuddly, fuzzy blue creature he most definitely was not.

Nor could she bear to call him by that other—awful—name, Blake, that brought with it such vivid reminders of humiliation, anger and embarrassment. So, swallowing hard and praying her mother had suffered a serious memory loss since their last conversation about Annie's "new guy," she said, "This is Sean Murphy."

Sean's brow went up in surprise, as if thinking she'd goofed up. When he opened his mouth to correct her—what was he going to say, "Sorry, she forgot my name on the ride up here?"—she shook her head in warning.

Her father was courteous enough to smile politely and extend his hand. Steve, the middle son and prankster, circled around her and whispered, "He's got an earring. Is it on the right side?"

Knowing immediately what he meant, Annie smirked, "Sorry, big brother, your loss. Let's just say I have absolutely no doubts about his sexual preferences."

"You're *so* funny." He swatted her, then greeted Sean, as did Randy. And every man in her family had something to say about the fat cat currently sprawled like a twenty pound sack of potatoes over Sean's left shoulder.

"Why is everybody picking on my Wally?"

Jed looked at her as if she was foolish. "Because he's meaner than the bull in the south pasture."

Before she could argue it, her mother stepped out of the house, onto the porch, then raced down the stairs. Annie planted her feet firmly on the ground, knowing she was in for an exuberant bear hug, which she got.

They stood outside talking for a few minutes, during which she got the rundown on the latest happenings of the entire Davis clan.

With grandparents, aunts, uncles and cousins spread throughout the encircling three counties, there was lots of news to catch up on. Who was engaged. Who was pregnant. Who had disappointed his parents by getting suspended for letting a whole bunch of chickens loose in the high-school gymnasium. Who had shot his toe off while doing some out-of-season hunting, and didn't that just serve him right?

The usual.

Through it all, Sean maintained a smile, stroked the cat, responded politely when addressed. And maintained a tall, solid presence beside her that reminded Annie she was *not* alone. They were in this together. For better or for worse.

And what a wonderful feeling it was.

"Oh, listen to me jabbering away," her mother finally said when she'd run out of wind. "Let's go inside and relax. The food's almost done, you must be famished from the long drive."

Famished, yes. But not for food.

When she caught Sean's eye and saw the twinkle in there, she knew he'd done that mind-reading thing again. Unable to keep herself from touching him, she reached for his hand, twined her fingers in his, and led him up the steps.

Answering the fresh litany of questions as they walked inside the house, Annie offered Sean a look that both apologized…and offered to make this up to him.

If they survived it.

SEAN LIKED ANNIE'S family. All of them. But he especially liked her mother.

He suspected the woman looked just like Annie would in thirty years. Slim and energetic, her short hair was more of an ash-blond, and she had laugh lines beside her pretty blue eyes.

Though she was talkative, and fussed over her only daughter, Mrs. Davis was also calm and straightforward about the way she ruled the family. Her husband and sons might not realize it, but the woman was entirely in charge. She got everyone to do exactly what she wanted with the lift of a brow or the gesture of a hand, which he found terribly amusing, given the size of the men she was ordering about.

Once or twice, she'd caught his eye, noted his amusement, and grinned impishly at him. As if the two of them already shared a secret.

In the two hours since they'd arrived, Annie's family had had so much to say to her that they'd pretty well left him alone, beyond the usual niceties. And he'd enjoyed the big country brunch, the likes of which he hadn't eaten since his Irish breakfast days.

He'd wager Wally, who'd taken up residence beneath Annie's chair, had liked it, too. Judging by the number of times Annie slipped him a nibble of this or that, he had to be in spoiled cat heaven.

Annie's older brothers had departed for their own homes after eating, so that pressure was off. The younger brother was an energetic puppy. The barrel-chested, gray-haired father remained cordial, if not enthusiastic. He'd had a newspaper in front of his face since the moment he'd finished his meal, so there was no pressure there. And Annie's mother had been friendly since the moment they'd arrived.

So he'd have to say things had been going quite well. For the most part.

They were a very nice family…but not *entirely* welcoming, he had to admit. Because all of them had, at one point or another, said *something* to make it clear that Annie belonged here, with them, not in some big city with anybody else.

He got the message. He was wearing an *Anybody* sign around his neck.

Still, with two brothers gone, the father distracted and the mother chattering about tonight's party, Sean had begun to let his guard down.

Obviously too soon.

"So, Sean, where exactly did you and Annie meet?"

The pointed look in Mrs. Davis's eye said she was ready to get down to business. The grill-the-new-boyfriend business.

Sean's mind went blank as his hostess addressed him. Trying desperately to remember what they'd agreed upon—dating service? blind date?—he opened his mouth. But his answer was cut short when Annie said, "We met at a party."

He nodded. "Right. A party." Being creative, he embellished a little bit. "A Halloween party."

Mr. Davis peered over the top of his paper, his brow pulled into a small frown. "I thought Annie said you'd only been seeing each other a couple of months."

Foot meet mouth. Damn.

"Well, *dating,* yes, but we've known each other longer."

The lie came easily off Annie's lips. Normally, he'd expect seeing someone make up such falsehoods so easily would be a turn-off. Instead, he wanted to commend her for being so quick on her feet. The gleam of humor in her eyes over their shared secret amused him to no end.

She was good at this subterfuge thing. One of James Bond's babes couldn't have been any more creative.

Sean smothered a sigh, thinking of the *Bond* thing. That had come up almost as soon as he'd arrived. And again at least once an hour since.

Why, oh why, could Americans not hear the difference between an Irish accent and an English one?

"Being friends with someone you date is a very smart idea," Mrs. Davis said, nodding in approval. "Sooner or later the blind excitement wears off and it's nice to be with someone you actually *like* when it does."

The paper shook slightly, and Mr. Davis's voice emerged from behind it. "Blind excitement…riiiight."

Judging by his long, deep sighs whenever the subject of tonight's anniversary party came up, Mr. Davis wasn't quite the romantic his wife was. He seemed the type to keep his head down and his mouth closed, obviously used to doing just that after thirty-five years of marriage to such a powerful woman.

Right now, he also seemed to be completely distracted and separate from the conversation going on around him. But Sean had no illusions that the man was paying very careful attention to his daughter and the new guy.

"Sean was just so nice and charming, we hit it off from the minute we met," Annie said, holding her mother's gaze with complete innocence.

She wasn't lying, not at all. They *had* hit it off right

away. Only, it had happened five days ago. Not eight months ago.

Having lived in his own veil of half-truths, and knowing the benefits of discretion, he didn't hold it against her. Just because Sean liked her family so far, that didn't mean he hadn't seen *exactly* what she'd been warning him about from the minute her oldest brother had rapped him on the back of the head.

They were close-knit, incredibly protective, and while well-mannered, there had been more than one under-the-breath comment about Sean "stealing" their little girl away. As if he had anything to do with her having left home, what was it, *five* years ago?

The nonstop commentary about friends, family and neighbors and the not-very-subtle assumption that Annie would be back when she got over her "little adventure" was grating on him after two hours. He simply couldn't imagine what it was like for her each and every time she spoke to any of them.

No, he didn't blame her for her tiny white lies. If his presence here could get them to at least address the possibility that Annie might *not* be moving home, next year, or the following one at the very latest, then he was very glad to do it.

"What was she dressed as?" Randy asked. Annie's youngest brother was a typical gangly twenty-year-old, all arms, legs and mouth, with a shaggy head full of blond hair. He yucked it up asking, "Lemme guess— Little Orphan Annie? That's what I used to call her."

Mrs. Davis was walking by the table to refill a platter of waffles and she paused midstride to thwack her youngest son on the head with the back of her hand. "And what would that make your father and me if your sister was an orphan?" She then made the sign of the cross and mumbled what sounded like a prayer before proceeding to the stove.

Sean made no effort to hide his smile.

"Actually, she looked wonderful," he told her brother, wondering if Annie recognized the mischief in his tone. "She was a bunny."

Randy snorted. "Yeah, right, Annie a *Playboy* bunny?"

Seeing her mother swing around in dismay, and Mr. Davis lower the newspaper and frown, Sean quickly shook his head. "Heavens, no. Annie wore a big, pink, fuzzy thing with floppy ears and painted on whiskers." He winked at her. "She was quite adorable."

Her glare promised retribution. Her words delivered it. "Oh, yes, and Sean was dressed up as Fred Flintstone. He looked very macho as a caveman. Can't you just see the resemblance?"

Caveman? Heaven forbid. But, fair was fair. He couldn't really expect her to describe him as a sexy Zorro or wicked pirate when he'd painted such a vivid picture of her bouncing about as the Easter Bunny.

"That does sound macho," Mrs. Davis said with a grin as she returned to the table, carrying a fresh pot of coffee. "Are you sure you won't have some, Sean?"

"Sean drinks tea, Mom."

Good memory.

"But Annie drinks enough coffee for both of us," he said, laughing and giving her an intimate look. "Takes a lot to get her going in the morning."

Her eyes widened into twin saucers. He immediately backpedaled.

"If I call her before she's had her second cup of the day, she sounds as though she's sleepwalking."

Good save, she mouthed when her mother turned to reach for the sugar bowl.

When she turned back around, sprinkling a spoonful of sugar into her cup, Mrs. Davis casually murmured, "You know, Annie, I'd been meaning to ask you." Her barely interested tone didn't fool Sean one bit. He prepared himself for whatever was coming, already realizing Mrs. Davis was far more intuitive than any of the male members of the family. "I was certain you'd said Sean's name was something else when you first mentioned him to me on the phone."

Beside him, Annie stiffened in her chair. Sean reached over and dropped a hand on her bare leg, the intimate touch hidden from view by the dish-laden table. He *had* this one.

"We have cute nicknames for each other," he said. "Maybe that's what you remember."

Her mother didn't look convinced.

"What's Annie's?" Randy asked.

Her hand dropped to cover the one he had on her leg, squeezing him threateningly. Her sudden glare promised extreme retribution. He sensed that if he told her family he called her Honey Bunny or Flopsy Ears—which, as nauseating as they sounded, made sense given the way they'd *supposedly* met—she'd crown him with the platter of congealing fried ham.

And if he called her his little cottontail, her father might.

"I call her *céadsearc*," he murmured. Wanting to reassure her that everything was fine, he couldn't resist lifting her hand and brushing his lips across her fingers. "It means sweetheart."

The father retreated behind the newspaper again. The twenty-year-old snickered with typical youthful disdain of anything the slightest bit mushy.

But the mother? She stared at their joined hands, ob-

viously noted the warm, grateful look in Annie's eye—
and the tender one Sean couldn't contain, and said,
"How lovely."

And Sean knew he'd won over the most important
person in the house.

He lowered his hand to the surface of the table,
keeping his fingers wound with Annie's. "That she is."

Mrs. Davis smiled at him, slowly nodded, then
looked away. Before she did so, he'd swear he saw
moisture in her eyes. Though, he had to be mistaken.
Didn't mothers want their daughters to find men who
truly cared about them?

Maybe. But in this case, with a mother who wanted
her daughter to give up her dreams and come
home…maybe not.

"So, sad-sac," Randy asked, mangling the endearment, "what's yours for him?"

Annie wrinkled her nose at the younger man. "It's
Noneya. As in none-ya business. Now go away and do
some push-ups or something before you overtax your
brain with all this adult conversation."

"Can't. Gotta get ready for the game."

Beside him, he felt Annie stiffen, even before she
said a word. His guard immediately went up.

"No."

"Oh, yeah, it's Saturday."

She leaned around him to glare at her brother. "We
have enough to do getting ready for the party tonight."

"That's not necessary, dear." Mrs. Davis helped
herself to another waffle, then put one on Mr. Davis's
plate. He didn't even put the paper down, merely
reached blindly for some syrup, doused it liberally, then
cut a piece off with the side of his fork. "Everything's
all ready. You and Sean can just enjoy yourselves."

"We won't enjoy ourselves if those three idiots give Sean a concussion."

"Uh," he asked, "what exactly is it we're talking about here?"

"The game," Randy replied. He reached over, scooped a handful of bacon, and rose from the table. "Every Saturday at three, after the milking's done and the deliveries are made, whoever's around meets on the back field for some football. We do it all summer." He popped food into his mouth and spoke around it. "It's fun."

"It's violent," Annie snapped. "How many Saturday trips to the hospital does this family have to make before that stupid tradition stops?"

Her father muttered, "I'm not paying any more dental bills, boy. If you lose any more of your teeth, you'll be gumming your food long before you're ninety."

Good God, losing teeth in a friendly afternoon game at the house? No wonder Annie's older brothers had left. They'd gone home to suit up in their armor and to put on helmets to bash him in the head with, rather than just the backs of their hands.

"Everybody expects you to play," Randy said, ignoring his sister and his father. "You know how, right? I mean, I know they don't play it in England. There, they call soccer football, right? Which is stupid, why don't they just call it soccer since football is already football?"

His head hurting a little from the young man's confused logic, he started with the basics. "I'm Irish," he explained. *Again.* "And I can only speculate that it made sense to someone to call a game involving your feet and a ball *football*. As opposed to the game *you* play, which mostly involves passing and throwing and *carrying* the ball, and which has all that protective padding and the constant time-outs."

Annie snorted, and from behind the paper, he'd swear he heard a chuckle.

Randy didn't even appear to notice that his logic was being questioned. "But you know how to play? Or do you just play the sissy English version?"

Sean shouldn't have let a twenty-year-old pup get a rise out of him. But his competitive spirit was rearing up. "Ever heard of rugby?"

Randy's eyes narrowed. "Is that the one where the guys all bend over head to butt and hug each other to decide who gets the ball?"

Sean barked a laugh, remembering the many injuries, bruises and breaks he'd suffered during his university days. "Yes, that's the one."

"You don't have to do this," Annie murmured.

"It'll be fun," he said. Seeing a flash of worry on her face, he quickly added, "I'll be fine."

Her response completely surprised him. Leaning close, she whispered, "It's not you I'm worried about. You told me you've knocked men unconscious on the field, remember? If you give one of my brothers a concussion, you might be sleeping in the barn tonight."

Neither of them realized they'd been overheard. Not until another of those low, dry chuckles emerged from behind the newspaper. And her father, who must not think too highly of the Saturday afternoon tradition spoke.

"I'll put twenty bucks on the Irishman."

9

"YOUR PARENTS SEEMED very happy tonight."

Annie, who was curled sideways in the passenger seat of Sean's rental car, watching the way the warm summer breeze lifted his hair back as they drove through the night, nodded and smiled. "Yes, they did. I think they were surprised to see how many people care about them and wanted to share their big day."

It was after eleven and the two of them had just left the Elks Lodge, which was on the outskirts of Green Hills, about five miles from the farm. The party, which started at six, had finally wound down until only Davis family members, both close and extended, remained. Seeing Annie's yawn—after the long day and the drive to town, as well as Sean's, after the long day, the drive *and* the testosterone-laden football game—her mother had insisted that they head back to the house early.

Good thing. Randy had nearly lost his mind when he'd seen Sean's car. He'd begged to ride with them, and when Anne had told him the Ferrari was only a two-seater, Randy had insisted that his sister wouldn't mind riding with someone else to the party. She sensed the return trip wouldn't have been any different.

And there was no *way* she was riding with somebody else. Not when she'd been unable to take her hungry eyes off the man sitting beside her throughout the entire evening.

Just like almost every other woman there.

"Thanks for not getting upset about my cousin Elizabeth fawning all over you," she said. "At fourteen, she hasn't quite learned the art of keeping her feelings to herself."

Sean glanced at her from the corner of his eye. "I'd say that runs in the family."

Still too lazily comfortable and happy just watching him, she took no offense. Because it was true. She was utterly incapable of holding back a thing, especially when it came to the things she wanted.

Right now, she had no doubt about what she most wanted. All she had to do was study the strong lines of his face, the perfectly curved mouth, the strength of his jaw, and her body told her with hard, pulsing insistence what she wanted. And when she dropped her gaze to the broad shoulders, the lean hips and the long legs, the moisture between her thighs told her even more.

"Thank *you* for not getting mad about your brother's black eye."

She snickered. "I'd have been more mad if Jed had done any damage to you in that stupid game. And hearing Dad's laughter—seeing the look on his face when you wiped the field with all of them—was almost enough to make this entire trip worthwhile. Even the five thousand dollars."

Hell, the five thousand dollars had been more than made up for already. Last night…in the ball pit. And on her desk.

"Well, I hope we can find one or two more pleasant things to do to make this trip worthwhile," he said, a slight smile on those full, kissable lips.

Oh, she had no doubt they could if they had the opportunity. But they wouldn't be able to explore those options back at the house, which would be bursting with other Davises in a very short time.

Arriving home first, they'd have a *little* privacy at the house, but not enough to risk doing the kinds of things Annie wanted to do. And while she suspected her mother had sent them off early specifically because she knew the two of them were having a hard time keeping their hands off each other in public, she also knew the older woman wouldn't give them too long.

So go somewhere else.

The idea had merit. They could take a detour for some intimate, alone time. They were a good half-hour ahead of everyone else, and no one would be looking for them right away.

A half-hour wasn't nearly enough. But if it was all she could get tonight, damn it, she'd take it.

"Turn right up ahead," she said, suddenly remembering some of the party spots she and her high-school friends had discovered along the back roads.

"Are you sure? That seems too soon."

It wasn't soon enough. Not nearly. For the past five hours, she'd been dying to shove all her cousins and friends away from this man and wrap herself around him like an octopus. So getting him somewhere private where she could jump on him couldn't *possibly* come soon enough.

"I'm sure," she whispered.

Sean glanced at her, obviously hearing the intimate tone. He smiled slowly, then turned his attention back toward the road. He followed her directions, and, as she expected, within a few minutes they found themselves leaving the blacktop for a gravel-and-dirt lane. One that, if she recalled correctly, went absolutely nowhere.

"Hey, navigator, you paying attention over there?"

Reaching over, she slid her fingers into his hair, curling a few strands around them. "Keep going."

He nodded, licking his lips, his knowing expression easily visible in the reflection of the dashboard lights. The way he shifted in his seat, stretching his legs, tugging his trousers, told her his mind had gone in the same direction as hers. They were driving toward carnal pleasures and they both knew it.

Soon after leaving the main road—and the few streetlights—behind them, they were traveling down a windy, tree-shaded lane. Darkness had almost completely enveloped them. They were entirely alone, a few miles from any building, surrounded by fields and pastures. Only local farmers used this road by day, and no one had any reason to use it at night.

It was good enough. Separated from the rest of the world by distance and trees and fields and darkness, they could finally give in to the pulsing hunger that had been dancing between them. It had been banked, put away since their last deep, wet kiss to mark their mutual orgasms the night before in her office. Now they were going to have a chance to let their hunger come out and play in the moonlight.

"I want that moonlight," she whispered. She looked up at the canopy of trees above the open roof of the convertible, seeing only glimpses of golden light here and there where the thick leaves left occasional gaps.

Too dark. Annie knew she wouldn't be satisfied with frantic, frenzied blind touches. She wanted to see him. To experience everything. This road would not do.

"Up ahead there's a small dirt path. Turn right."

He didn't question her again, but leaned forward in his seat, as if silently urging the car to get to their destination more quickly on the windy, unmarked road.

"This third-date rule of yours," he asked as he carefully took the appropriate turn, onto a lane even more rough and narrow than the one they'd been traveling. "Is it like one-two-three, *then* go? Or do you go *on* three?"

Unable to believe the man could make her laugh when she was a bundle of oversexed nerves, she replied, "In case you forgot, we kind of threw the third-date rule out the window last night."

"Oh, I hadn't forgotten, darlin'." He grabbed her hand, still twined in his hair, and brought her fingers to his mouth. Lightly biting the tip of one, he murmured, "But I honestly considered last night more of a quick appetizer." He shook his head. "No, not even that…just an hors d'oeuvre. If this is the official end of the waiting, we're going to be having a nine-course *feast.*"

She shivered, getting the picture. He was right. There was so much they hadn't done last night. And she was every bit as anxious to do them as Sean.

In thirty minutes?

Hell. Maybe the family would stay longer. When they left, her Great Aunt Trudy had been winding up to tell stories about her old USO days. That could go on for ages.

Besides, it was her parents' anniversary. Surely they wouldn't wait up for her, like they had when Annie was a teenager. And deep in her heart, she hoped they still had the kind of intimate marriage that would demand that they slip away to their room for a private celebration. Even if she *so* didn't want to think about the details.

"Here!" she said, realizing they'd just reached the perfect spot. The dirt lane had curved up through the woods, coming out at the top of a hill. They burst from beneath the trees like a train emerging from a dark tunnel.

Though entirely deserted and uncultivated, the area had been cleared long ago. Nothing came between the moonlight and their bodies. No shadows to interfere with their visual enjoyment of each other. Nothing but the night breeze faintly stirring the dry grass all around them. And the two of them, Annie and Sean, sitting beneath a glorious umbrella of midnight blue sky dotted with a million sparkling stars.

"Beautiful spot," Sean said, looking down at the vista falling away from the front of the car, and then up at the universe spread in an artist's palette above them.

She could have agreed, could have talked about the view. But those thirty minutes were pushing her, and the hunger she'd suppressed for the past twenty-four hours was rising up from deep inside, ready to consume her. She hadn't brought this man out here on what could be their last full night together to admire the view.

He reached for her. "Annie…"

She didn't hesitate, sliding one leg over his lap to straddle him in the driver's seat. Twining her fingers in his hair, she covered his mouth with hers, her tongue plunging wildly, demanding his attention. He gave it, tasting her just as deeply, just as intensely. With his hands on her hips, he pulled her so tight against his rock-hard erection she couldn't even move.

Well, not much. She moved a little—up and down, rubbing on him, needing the sensation there…and, oh, God, *there.*

"Not tonight," he growled, holding her still, keeping her from riding him anymore. "I said a nine-course feast, darlin', not a fast-food drive-thru."

"The time…"

"Fuck the time, Annie." He buried his face in her throat, scraping his teeth along her collarbone. "I'm having you, I'm having all of you. And if we show up at your parents place in three hours with your hair a mess, red marks on your throat, my fingerprints on your thighs and your lipstick on my pants, I honestly won't give a damn."

Red marks…fingerprints…and, oh, lipstick. What a delicious litany of images flashed through her mind. She wanted all of the above. As many times as she could get them in the short time they had.

Short time. Tonight. Tomorrow. That's all.

Annie pushed the hurtful thought away. She didn't want to even consider that a period she'd begun to think could be the most amazing time in her life could be over almost as quickly as it had begun. Or that she'd wasted the first few days of it with silly rules about third dates.

Almost desperate to take what she could, Annie kissed him again, tasting in lazy thrusts this time. Without even breaking the connection, she felt Sean reach for the door handle and open it. Annie immediately took advantage, sliding her cramped right leg down and out.

She'd assumed he'd been making her more comfortable. She did *not* expect him to encircle her waist and step out of the car, his hands under her butt, her legs wrapping around his hips. "Sean?"

"Slight change of position," he muttered. Not explaining, he turned them around, backing her into the car this time. But instead of pushing her down onto the seat he'd just left, he lifted her higher, positioning her on the back hood, with her bare legs dangling down inside the car, resting against the two seats. Then he parted them.

Mmm. Much better. "I like the way you think."

His eyes glittered. "You're really going to like this."

He knelt on the seats in front of her, his face level with her middle. Annie looked down at him, running the tips of her fingers along the moonlit highlights in his hair, watching as he began to unbutton her blouse from the bottom up.

With every button he unfastened, he kissed a spot of the skin he uncovered. Starting at her belly. Moving up, over her midriff. To the under-curves of her breasts.

"Sean," she groaned, wishing he could hurry up, wanting his mouth and his hands and that incredible erection she'd had deep inside her body the night before.

If he stood on the seats, she could have it right where she most wanted it. She could taste and lick and suck until he was as out of his mind as anyone could possibly get.

Annie wasn't the queen of oral sex. But if desire was enough, she knew she could pleasure this man until he wouldn't be able to remember his own name.

He wouldn't be rushed, however. Not this time.

"You are so beautiful," he whispered. "For the rest of my life, I will never again smell peaches without thinking of you." He pushed the blouse off her shoulders, letting it fall to the lid of the trunk. "Of this."

He unfastened the front clasp of her bra between one slow stroke of his tongue against her cleavage and the next. And when it fell away, he moved that tongue, that incredible mouth, to her pebbled nipple. But before tasting her, giving her the intimate kiss she needed, he scraped the side of his rough cheek against it. Annie quivered and reflexively clenched her legs together, wondering how a little touch on one small part of her body could spread to every other inch of her. His lean hips were between her legs, so she couldn't clench far—just enough to hold him tight and keep him there.

He finally licked the aching tip of one breast, his flat tongue providing a smooth, velvety caress. The taste left moisture in its wake, which the night breeze rolled across to make her shiver. "Please, Sean."

"Shh, let me. Just let me."

She let him.

Knowing just when to give, and when to move away, Sean made thorough love to her breasts. He caressed her, stroked her, filled his hands with her. Suckling one nipple, rubbing the other between his fingertips, he soon had her shaking and thrusting against his lower body. Annie was so wet and aroused she could barely stand the pressure of the hard car against her most intimate parts.

It was a long while before he backed up enough to let her pull his shirt off. Once it was gone, she busied herself stroking the long lines of thick muscle on his shoulders and his upper back. His body was slick with a light coating of sweat caused, she suspected, by the amazing restraint, the efforts he made to keep complete control over what was happening.

"I like your skirt," he whispered as he worked his way down again. "I've been wondering all evening what you had on underneath it."

He was about to find out, and she could hardly wait. But instead of undressing her completely and exploring her that way, he instead touched her through the cloth. He lightly traced the outline of her hip bone and his mouth soon followed his fingers.

Annie couldn't help thrusting up, at least a little, inviting him to go farther. Not, she suspected, that he needed any such invitation. Sean was going to take what he wanted tonight, he'd made that very clear.

The certainty that he wanted to use his mouth on her, to drive her to madness with those lips and that tongue, had her ready to fall off the car in pure shivers of excitement.

He laughed softly at her desperate efforts to demand more, but he didn't give in. Still taking his damn sweet time, he moved lower. Tasting, sampling, he heightened the tension even by simply rubbing his cheek against her clothes, but denying her the connection of his mouth on her skin.

He knew that he was driving her mad, and Annie honestly wasn't sure whether she wanted to thank him or bash him in the head for it.

Finally, the tips of his fingers went lower, pressing the soft fabric against the swollen lips of her sex. Sean's mouth quickly followed, and he kissed her softly, gently, as if he was kissing her mouth.

Annie wriggled, shocked by how good it felt. She'd never experienced anything like it. Any previous experience she'd had with oral sex had always been more a perfunctory reciprocation or a quick, guaranteed bit of foreplay designed only to lead to something else. A tongue jabbing at her clit so her lover could check that off his list and move on.

This was leading to nothing else. Nothing but her deep-rooted pleasure.

She dropped her head back, looked up at the stars and let him pleasure her. He was so slow, every exhaled breath a deliberate stroke of air flowing across her most sensitive spot. And every inhalation an audible appreciation of the musky scent of her body.

"You taste so good, Annie."

Sean wrapped his hands around her waist, tugging her forward just a little, tilting her so he could delve more deeply into her secrets. With an appreciative groan, he flattened his tongue and licked her right through the flimsy layers of clothes. She gasped as warm, liquid want sluiced to her crevice.

Finally, when she thought she'd go mad with the almost-there touches, Sean pushed her skirt up. He revealed her thighs an inch at a time, kissing his way up her legs. He didn't pause when he reached her panties. Instead, he merely tugged them out of the way with his fingertips, and, without warning, plunged his tongue deep into her.

Annie screamed, jerking up toward him, shocked by how intimate it was. How incredibly erotic.

He slid his tongue in and out, making love to her, something no man had ever done. When he had her good and dripping, Sean moved up to attend to her clit, delicately tasting, swirling around it rather than attacking And she came in a hot bolt of pleasure almost immediately.

She barely noticed when he tugged her clothes off and tossed them to the seat. But she definitely noticed when he removed his own. Because in the low light, his body was godlike, huge and powerful, almost pagan beneath the full summer moon.

His sex jutted out proudly in front of him, and she went warm and liquid inside, wanting to be filled by it. But she also wanted to taste it—to give him a little of the madness he'd given her. So, without asking, she bent down and licked at its tip, catching the moisture there on her tongue.

He hissed.

"Only fair," she murmured, "that I get a turn."

He said nothing, watching her from above as she sampled him again, licking, rubbing lightly. Until finally she stretched her mouth wide and took as much of him as she could manage.

Sean's hands twined in her hair, his body responding with a slow thrust that appeared completely beyond his control.

Annie took the thrust, swallowed him deeper, laved him with her tongue. Her hands on his lean hips, she dug her fingertips into his tight butt, helping him set a rhythm she could handle. Then she urged him with strokes and groans to do what he wanted, to take whatever he needed.

He didn't last long, only a minute or two. Then with a low groan, he pushed her away, tugging her back up until they were face-to-face. She hadn't even had a chance to catch her breath before he covered her mouth and kissed her deeply.

He'd apparently tucked a condom into his pocket before they'd left the house. Or else he merely traveled with them. Annie didn't know, didn't care, she was just blissfully grateful he had one.

Watching him tear it open, she reached down to take it from his hands, wanting to feel the silky-skinned column of heat before it was encased.

"Annie," he warned her as she wrapped her hand around him, tight, stroking up and down.

"I'm going to be coming if you keep that up."

Yeah, right. From what she'd seen of him the night before, the man would be a long time coming.

Annie could hardly wait.

When he was sheathed, she parted her legs more, tugging him closer, wetting him with her body's juices. "Take me, Sean."

"We're getting there," he murmured, not doing as she asked. Instead he pushed her back a little, began to kiss and suckle her breasts again. And it wasn't until she was panting and arching into his mouth—demanding it harder, deeper, more intense—that he finally eased into her body with a slow, steady thrust.

"Yes!"

She slid down to meet him, pressing her pelvis hard against his, taking it all. And then staying very still, savoring the penetration, not wanting to budge for fear it would be over too soon.

She should have known better. Because, still in complete control, Sean began to move. He whispered sweet things in her ears and kissed her hair as he slowly filled her, then retreated. When the tension increased, he twined his fingers in that hair and muttered his need in a coarse, hungry demand, plunging hard and fast.

She couldn't have chosen which she liked more. She liked it all. Wanted it all. And took it all.

Until after what seemed like forever, they both cried out their climaxes to the stars and collapsed down to the seat of the car.

THEY WEREN'T ABLE to say their final goodbyes and get on the road until noon on Sunday. Sean would have liked nothing better than to have left at the crack of dawn and been back in Chicago by eight o'clock. Then to go straight to his hotel and make love to Annie for a good twenty-four hours.

After that, well, he honestly didn't know. He was

supposed to leave tomorrow, supposed to board a jet and fly to Hong Kong. He had a meeting on Wednesday, people were counting on him.

But leaving her... God, why did the very idea *hurt* so much? Personal relationships had never hurt him, aside from the odd twinge of sadness over missing his little sister. But the sharp ache inside him at the thought of exiting Annie's life as quickly as he'd entered it was enough to double him over.

"Thank you again for your hospitality," Sean said to Mr. Davis after he'd put Annie's bag in the car. "It was nice meeting you all." He grinned at Annie's three brothers. "Next time, I'll teach you how to play rugby."

Jed, who still sported a black eye from yesterday's supposedly low-contact, friendly game, nodded. "Yeah, we're definitely due for another round." The glare might have been threatening, but his tone held a note of respect.

The entire family had walked them to the car, Rex and Radar following the procession like a pair of royal guards. He supposed it was their own fault that the morning had dragged on so long—he and Annie hadn't got back to the house until two in the morning and they'd overslept. So the whole family had been able to arrive in time for the big farewell scene.

"You drive safe now," Mr. Davis said as Sean helped Annie into her seat. "Wear your..."

"I'm on it, Dad," she said, already buckling herself in.

The look in his eye said he wouldn't apologize for trying to keep her safe. Sean recognized it, having seen it on the face of his own father. Not just toward Moira, either. His old man had often visibly worried about Sean's safety growing up.

That his father loved him had never been anything Sean had questioned. Any more than the certainty that Annie's family loved her.

How they showed that love, though, was quite different. Because despite the under-the-breath comments, there had been no scenes, no pleading, no threats or demands. They didn't like the life she'd chosen...but they weren't about to try to force her to change it.

His father could learn something from them.

"Give us a call and let us know you made it home okay, won't you?" Annie's mother asked as she bent to kiss her daughter on the cheek. Then the older woman stroked Annie's hair, and whispered something in her ear, something she obviously didn't want to share with the men of the family. She spoke quietly, obviously relaying more than just well-wishes and love.

From his seat beside her, Sean could feel the way Annie suddenly stiffened. Whatever her mother had said, she hadn't been expecting it.

Curious, he started the car, replied to the fresh shouts of goodbye, then drove down the long lane toward the main road. In the backseat, the cat immediately flung himself down and went to sleep. Annie, meanwhile, remained quiet, lost in thought for the first ten minutes of the ride. He let her be. If she wanted him to know what her mother had whispered, she'd tell him.

Apparently, she did. Because when they reached the highway, she finally said, "She knew."

"What?"

"My mother. She knew you weren't the man I'd been telling her about." She shook her head and reached under her sunglasses to rub at the corners of her eyes. "She knew you weren't Blake."

Sean started to chuckle, having already realized that

Mrs. Davis was a sharp one. But something about the way Annie said the name Blake gave him pause. Glancing over, seeing the quiver of her lips, and realizing she was genuinely distressed, he suddenly understood, as if a lightbulb had gone off over his thick head. "My God, there really *was* a Blake."

Annie didn't reply at first. Instead, she wearily removed her sunglasses, pushing them onto her head as if wanting him to see her eyes, to read the truth there.

If he hadn't already left the back road and entered a busy highway, he would have pulled over to do exactly that. But as it was, he kept his face forward, waiting for her to say whatever it was she was trying to find the words for.

"Yes," she finally admitted, "there *was* a Blake."

His jaw flexing, he strove to remain detached, impersonal. She had, after all, hired him for this weekend. So he shouldn't have expected her to be honest about what the hell was really going on. Or to be wounded now when he found out she had not.

"I see. He was your last lover?" God, he hated using that word in connection with anyone else who'd ever touched Annie.

"No. Not my lover."

It wasn't until he released his breath in a slow whoosh that he realized he'd been holding it, waiting for her to answer.

"We dated, but it had never gone that far."

The dull tone in her voice told him it had gone far enough. Far enough to wound, to hurt. Far enough to leave a scar.

Forcing his own feelings out of the mix, he reached for her hand and twined his fingers with hers. "What happened?"

"He was married."

Stunned, Sean couldn't help gritting his teeth. Annie didn't seem the type. She was so honest, so open and sweet.

Not that he was about to pass judgment, not given his own history. Jesus, many of the women he'd been with had been the bored wives of husbands who'd paid Sean to keep them company.

Still, the idea of Annie being a part of anything like that stung. Deeply. "I see."

She released his hand, as if feeling him draw away, if only mentally. "No, you don't. I didn't know he was married."

Annie went on to tell him the whole story, speaking quickly, and every word she said increased his anger. By the time she'd finished, his hands were clenched so tightly around the steering wheel they actually hurt.

"So he used his baby boy to get in your good graces, to soften you up for the poor abandoned father. Then tried to lie his way into your bed."

"Pretty much."

Son of a bitch. Sean would like to have his tight hands around the man's throat, rather than this impersonal padded wheel. This Blake deserved to be throttled by someone who knew how to do the job.

"I'm sorry I didn't tell you the truth," she admitted. "It's just very humiliating. I'm ashamed and embarrassed."

"And horrified at the very prospect of your parents finding out," he said, knowing instantly that it was true.

"Oh, you've no idea!"

Having just spent a weekend with the Davises, he had a very *good* idea. "What exactly did your mother say?"

Annie sniffed a little, then chuckled, as if not sure whether to cry or laugh with the relief of having gotten the whole sordid story off her chest. "She told me she couldn't think of a single 'nickname' that sounded like Blake."

Yeah, that hadn't been his best cover.

"And that while she didn't appreciate the deception…"

"Yes?"

Clearing her throat, she admitted, "She said judging by the way you and I looked at each other, there were real feelings between us, and she thought we could be very happy together."

Real feelings. Very happy. Together. Him and Annie. As in, happy as a couple, a genuine one. Marriage, family, a home. All the things he'd never envisioned for himself, things he'd been running from since the day he'd turned twenty-one.

And all were things he *knew* Annie truly wanted, on her own terms, after she'd seen the world.

Annie said nothing else. Instead she pulled her sunglasses back down over her eyes, and tilted her head back to let the hot sun fall onto her face, as if she wanted to take a nap.

In truth, she was giving him space, not forcing him to say a word. Not that he would have known what to say. So he merely continued to drive.

With every mile that passed beneath the wheels of the car, Sean felt the subtle pull of his *real* life. The closer they came to Chicago, the more that life drew him back, reminding him of the choices he'd made.

Choices that had seemed right at the time. But which now, with Annie's whispered words of a fantasy relationship he had never dreamed possible repeating in his ear, shamed him to his core.

10

ANNIE WASN'T SURE what to expect when they reached the city. Sean might take her back to his hotel as he'd sworn to do. He could be planning to make love to her in every way humans had ever tried until tomorrow morning when the sun came up.

Or, judging by the near silence—broken only by occasional small talk—in which they'd shared the two-hour ride, he might be ready to drop her off at her place. Some men might toss her cat and her suitcase on the sidewalk, and drive like hell to the airport.

She should have kept her mouth shut, should never have told him exactly what her mother had said. Honestly, though, the intuitive words had stunned Annie so much, she'd almost *had* to share them. If only to see whether saying them out loud made them any less shocking to her own ears.

Her mother had seen *love* in their eyes? Hers and Sean's? Was that even possible? After one week, could such a thing really happen?

In her mother's opinion, of course it could. She and Annie's father were a well-known case of love-at-first-sight. But those things didn't happen nowadays, did they? Especially not to women like Annie.

And *especially* not with men like Sean.

Arriving in the city, she almost held her breath to see

which way he'd go. When he turned toward his own hotel, rather than Lincoln Park, she somehow managed not to fall over and kiss his feet. Or to jabber her thanks for not yanking away these last hours they had with each other.

She wanted those hours. Wanted them desperately now that her mother's accusation had filled her brain with possibilities.

Not that she believed Sean loved her. But the idea that she, Annie, had truly fallen in love with him, suddenly didn't seem so ridiculous. In fact, she suspected it could be true. And knowing that, she wanted as much time with the man as she could get.

"I can't wait to explain the emu-prints on the hood of the car," Sean murmured, smiling for the first time in two hours. He'd just pulled into the garage beneath the hotel.

The garage…the one where she'd left her van.

Damn, maybe he'd brought her back here because he *had* to. She had to get her car, didn't she?

Parking, he reached into the backseat and picked up Wally's crate. She was sure he would kiss her goodbye and wave to her from the elevator. They couldn't very well traipse through the lobby of this five-star hotel with a fat, mean cat in a cage.

But it seemed that's exactly what he meant to do. Not even asking if she was coming up, he hoisted their two small bags over his shoulder, balancing the crate in his other hand, and walked toward the elevator. Not toward her own vehicle.

When she didn't follow right away, he looked back over his shoulder. "Annie?"

She swallowed hard and hurried to join him. "Coming."

Though she had no idea what he was thinking, or how he felt about what she'd said in the car, Sean was making it pretty clear that his plans for the rest of today—and tonight—hadn't changed. At the very least, they would have that much.

Beyond that? Well, she couldn't think about that now.

Almost giddy with relief, she followed him into the elevator and watched him punch the button for the lobby. Unfortunately, it appeared the elevator did not go straight up to his floor, so they were going to have to take Wally on tour.

"Are they going to let us bring him up?"

He shrugged, unconcerned. "If anyone has the nerve to try to stop us, I'll put down a pet deposit." He lifted the crate, eyeing Wally. "That means you have to be on your best behavior."

The idea that the cat would be refused simply didn't seem to occur to him. The man's self-confidence, his certainty of himself and what he was doing, poured off him. It was such a part of his personality that he didn't allow for any negative reaction to anything he did.

How amazing to be that confident. If Annie had that ability, she certainly wouldn't have had to go to a bachelor auction to find a date.

No way. She wouldn't have given up going to that auction for anything in the world.

"See? Nobody even noticed him," Sean said. They'd strolled with complete innocence through the massive lobby and down a short corridor leading to a bank of elevators going up to the rooms above.

"Thank God there wasn't a dog around, or they would have heard Wally screeching from the fortieth floor."

"Nah, he's a big pussycat, aren't you, boy?"

She was smiling over his cooing tone—the man could charm four-legged beasts as easily as the two-legged kind—when the elevator door in front of them opened with a quiet whoosh. Two women were inside, well-dressed ones carrying designer purses, with diamonds proclaiming their wealth around their necks and on their fingers.

Annie barely paid attention to them, at least until she felt Sean freeze beside her.

He didn't move. Didn't step inside, didn't get out of the way. Instead, he merely stared as one of the women—a very attractive brunette who was probably in her early forties—spied him and stepped so close their bodies almost touched.

"Sean!" the woman said, sounding completely delighted. Her smile tugged ten years off her face.

Oh, fabulous. An ex. As if they really needed something to bring back the tension that had finally seemed to be dissipating after the long car ride.

A tic appearing in his temple, Sean forced a smile of his own. "Constance."

"I had no idea you were stateside," the woman gushed. Then she looked down, saw the cage and the cat, and gaped. "You must be working for a *real* cat-woman this time, rather than just a catty one like me."

Annie, who had obviously become invisible—or was simply uninteresting enough to blend into the background—cleared her throat. "Sean, do you want me to take him so you can talk to your…friend?"

He met her stare, which was when she noticed that Sean *hadn't* turned to ice. No, there was heat in his eyes. Fiery heat. And *not* the kind he displayed when he looked at her with raw hunger.

His emotions were roiling inside him like the churning of a massive storm. Entirely foreign emotions—some she'd never associate with this man— oozed almost visibly from his every pore. She saw anger there. Embarrassment. Sadness.

Oh, God. This wasn't just an ex-girlfriend, she suddenly realized. He must have *loved* this woman. Though her comments about his working for someone were a little confusing. Had he gotten involved with his boss? Is that what had sent him into his current world-hopping career, which had no fixed address, no stability?

She reached for the cage.

"I've got him," Sean insisted, his words thick, his throat obviously tight.

"Sean?" the other woman said. Finally noticing Annie, his "friend" studied her closely. The assessing amber eyes noted the windblown hair, the off-the-rack T-shirt, the jean capris and the kick-around sandals.

They had absolutely no common ground, not a single thing that could make them relate to one another. Except the man standing between them.

"Oh," the wealthy woman finally murmured, blinking rapidly. Her face suffused with color, and she cleared her throat before turning her attention back to Sean. "I'm sorry. You…I mean…"

"It's all right," he bit out. "Nice to see you."

The woman nodded at him, then looked at Annie. "You've got a great guy," she said, her small smile appearing almost genuine. Then, grabbing her wide-eyed companion by the arm and tugging her away, she hurried down the hall and disappeared into the enormous lobby.

They stood in silence before the elevator door, which

had closed again. Sean made no move toward the call button, and she could almost see his mind working. As if he had to decide—proceed up to his room and pretend the interruption hadn't happened?

Or deal with it?

Almost afraid to know what he would tell her, Annie wasn't sure what she most wanted to happen. She still wasn't sure what he had decided when he finally reached over and pushed the Up button. Because he certainly didn't put his arm around her and tug her close, or kiss her lightly to reassure her that their afternoon would be proceeding exactly as they'd both expected it to.

Nor did he say a word all the way up to his floor, or even to his room.

Once inside, he dropped the bags and put the crate down. Opening it, he lifted Wally out, then finally turned his attention to Annie. And with six simple words, he clued her in on what he was planning to do.

"You might want to sit down."

GIVEN THE CHOICE between going home and walking into one of his father's surprise engagement parties, or telling Annie the truth about his past, Sean would willingly have booked a trip to Dublin right now. Because knowing the dismay—disgust—he was going to see in her eyes, proceeding was one of the hardest things he'd ever done.

But proceed he did.

"That woman…you're thinking she was a girlfriend."

Annie, who had taken his advice and sat on the plush sofa that took up the outer room of his two-room suite, nodded. "Yes." Shaking her head, she added, "Look, just because I told you about my sordid past doesn't mean we have to go sharing romantic stories."

"There's nothing romantic about this one."

She waited.

"In fact, my relationship with Constance, which lasted for about a week a few years ago in Munich, was entirely business."

"Did *she* know that?"

Though it was only the middle of the afternoon, Sean couldn't help opening the minibar. He needed a drink. And he wanted her to have one…because he had the feeling she'd soon need it, too.

But she declined with a brief shake of her head, waiting while he opened a small bottle and poured himself a shot of whiskey. Not particularly good whiskey, since it didn't come from Ireland, but it would do.

He finally answered her question. "Yes, she knew. Despite appearances, she's a very nice woman."

Annie nodded, not doubting it, obviously having seen the genuine regret in Constance's face over her faux pas. His former associate wasn't stupid—she'd taken one look at Annie and had realized that she'd stepped right into the middle of a very *personal* relationship. Because anyone could see that the beautiful young blonde sitting across from him would never need to hire any man to give her what she needed.

"She owns a gallery and had just gone through a bad divorce. She was in Munich attending some auctions, wanted someone to keep an eye on her and on her purchases…and hired me to be that someone."

Annie thought about it for a moment, her head tilting in obvious bewilderment. "You mean, you were her…bodyguard?"

"Yes, actually. That's what she asked me to be, at least at first."

"I'm confused. I thought you were a businessman."

He sipped his drink, then laughed harshly. "I'm in the *people* business, Annie. Wining and dining, wheeling and dealing, mostly for big corporations *these* days. But back then, my clients usually wanted something other than a good translator or negotiator."

"Like what?"

She still didn't get it. Didn't see the truth he was laying out in front of her.

So he made it a whole hell of a lot more clear.

"Like a lover."

She gasped.

"Though, love certainly had nothing to do with it. Attraction, yes. And money. But not love."

He saw the exact moment when understanding washed over her. Annie's pretty pink mouth trembled, then fell open in a nearly inaudible gasp. Her blue eyes grew huge in her face and her sun-kissed cheeks went pale.

Oh, yes, she understood.

Sean made no effort to explain, to backpedal his way out of the truth. Or even to make it clear that his business dealings now were much more normal and impersonal than they'd once been. Nor did he use the justification that he'd never had sex with a woman he wasn't attracted to, no matter what he was offered.

Because none of that mattered. The reality was, he'd done exactly what she thought he'd done.

"You were a prostitute."

He flinched. But didn't duck from the verbal stone. "Yes." Smiling with absolutely no humor, he clarified, "Though I preferred to be called a male escort at the time."

Annie rose, walked on shaky legs to the minibar, and helped herself to the bottle she'd refused before. She twisted the top off, brought the thing to her lips and drank straight from it, ignoring the clean glasses nearby.

When she was finished, she blinked a few times, cleared her throat, then met his stare. "So the auction last week. That wasn't such an unusual thing for you."

Feigning a nonchalance he didn't feel, Sean leaned one hip against the standard hotel-room desk and crossed his arms in front of his chest. "Actually, it was quite unusual. No woman ever paid five thousand dollars for an evening with me."

She frowned, then, understanding, muttered, "No, I imagine they paid a lot more."

The kind of women he'd been dealing with? Oh, yes. They most definitely had.

As if she couldn't bear to look at him, Annie crouched down, reaching out to her cat. Though usually aloof, the animal seemed to sense her need, because he immediately came to her, curling against her, letting himself be stroked by Annie's hand.

Her beautiful, vulnerable, *shaking* hand.

He turned away, unable to watch. Sean wanted to bend down and lift her to her feet, to kiss away her shock, to tell her the whole story—why he'd done it, what had driven him—everything.

Something stopped him. Maybe it was the way she'd repeated her mother's words in the car. Almost whispering, sounding stunned—and maybe a little wishful.

Sean couldn't make those wishes come true. Not now that she truly knew who he was…who he had been.

"I never expected to tell you any of this," he admitted. "Never dreamed there would be a reason."

She looked up, her eyes shiny with unshed tears. "And now there's a reason?"

"Yes. There is." That whole "cruel to be kind" motto had always annoyed him, but he suddenly knew that was the way this had to go down. He didn't want her crying over him, shedding a single tear. He simply wasn't worth it.

"I saw it in your eyes when you told me what your mother had said."

Her lashes lowered a little in pure self-defense.

"Don't mix up sex with emotion, Annie," he urged. "It's obvious you're a little confused, and considering what that asshole Blake did to you, that's pretty understandable. But you aren't in love with me."

He did not continue. Did not say the next natural sentence, *And I'm not in love with you either.*

Because Sean was many things, but he wasn't an outright liar. Saying that would, he believed, be lying not only to her but also to himself. Though he'd never completely understood the emotion, he knew what he was feeling for Annie was unlike anything he'd ever felt before. He wanted to be with her, wanted to make those dreams of hers come true, wanted all the things he'd been running away from for so long.

But when it came right down to it, she was just too damn good for him.

This way was best. It would end now, they'd both save face. They'd put their relationship back on a level they could both handle—that it had been a wild and wonderful fling, not soon forgotten, but nothing to write love songs and vows about. He'd walk out of her life, and she'd find someone else who fit into it much better than Sean Murphy ever could.

She finally rose to her feet, her throat visibly working as she swallowed down whatever emotion had risen up inside her. Her tone hard, she said, "I can separate sex from love."

It had worked. He'd hurt her, challenged her, and she'd reacted as he'd hoped she would. So why his throat felt as though he'd swallowed a mouthful of glass, he had no idea.

"But there's something you should know."

Seeing a sudden stiffening in her spine, he waited, wondering if he'd been congratulating himself—and mourning at the same time—a bit too soon.

"Despite what you think you know about me, I'm not easily shocked. And what you just told me…well, I don't like it, but I certainly can't hate you for things you did long before I ever met you."

"Don't you get it? Those things say a lot about who I am."

"Who you *were*," she clarified.

"Semantics."

She stepped close, brushing the tips of her fingers across his lips. "No, they're not. I don't know how many women you slept with in the past, but if you think I find it disgusting to imagine the number, well, you're wrong. Every single man I've met in Chicago has given it away for free to any women who'd let him."

"For free," he insisted, forcing the words through his clenched jaw.

She cupped that jaw in her hand, holding him still so he had to meet her eye. "I. Don't. Care."

Damn.

"I don't care about your past and I don't believe you truly think the choices you made when you were practically a kid have any genuine bearing on who you are now."

There she was wrong. At least, she was today. A week ago, he would have agreed with her. Now, though, feeling the awfulness of it—seeing the way her hand had shaken after he'd told her the truth about himself—oh, yes, it most definitely had bearing.

"I know what you're trying to do, and it won't work."

"What won't?"

"You won't convince me that you're an emotionless, oversexed user who is only out for money and self-gratification."

He thrust a frustrated hand through his hair, hearing tenderness in her tone. This was not going the way it was supposed to. Annie should be walking out the door right now.

"I don't know what you feel for me, but don't you dare tell me I don't know my own feelings toward you." Her voice shook with emotion. "I'm not saying we're going to live happily ever after, or that you'd ever even want to, but I sure as hell want to give it a try. Because I *am* falling in love with you, whether you want to believe it or not. And nothing you tell me about your past, your present or your future is going to change that."

He stared at her, saw the feelings she could not hide, heard the intensity—the certainty—in her voice. And knew she meant it. He was too late. She had fallen for him.

Jesus. This sweet, lovely, genuine woman had fallen in love with him. When he so completely didn't deserve it. He'd screwed up her life, almost as much as he'd screwed up his own.

"Let me love you," she whispered, rising on tiptoe to try to kiss him. "Let yourself love me."

He stepped back, shaking his head.

She followed. "Let it happen."

He remained as rigid as a statue. Maybe if he didn't care about her, if his emotions hadn't been as fully engaged as he believed they had, he could have been weak. Could have let her persuade him that the past could be forgotten and that he wasn't too sordid to associate with.

But he did care. Far too much to drag her down to his level.

"No, Annie. I'm sorry. I can't let it happen."

She was silent for a long, heavy moment, studying him, gauging the truth of his words. Acknowledging his resolve.

Then, after what seemed like ages, she stepped away and nodded once. "I understand."

At last.

Annie bent down and picked up her cat, tucking him into his cage, then grabbing her own overnight bag.

"Let me…"

She held a hand up, stopping him. "I'm fine." Turning on her heel, she walked to the door and put her hand on the knob. But before she twisted it, she spoke again, her words not much more than a heartfelt whisper.

"I'll be waiting."

And then she left.

_11_

THE FIRST LETTER arrived two weeks later.

Annie was sitting at her desk an hour after Baby Daze had closed. Everyone else had left, and she was sorting through bills, making up the next week's schedule. The usual.

Life had returned to normal, busy and fulfilling.

It was not happy. Not yet. Maybe she would be again, but getting over Sean wasn't proving to be the easiest thing she'd ever done. More like the most difficult.

But then she saw the white envelope with large, spiky black handwriting, addressed to her. It was postmarked from Paris.

And she began to have hope again.

"Sean," she whispered, touching the tip of her finger to her own scrawled name.

She'd heard nothing from him since that day in his hotel room, when he'd done his damndest to push her away. It had taken every ounce of her strength to let him do it, rather than continue to fight him. But in the end, she'd known she had to.

Only by letting him go—letting him come to terms with his own life—would she ever be able to hope he'd come back into hers.

Annie opened the envelope, and removed the single

sheet of paper within. Unfolding it, she read the first few words aloud, her own voice the only sound in the silent building.

"Dear Annie,
I am looking out my bedroom window, seeing through the evening mist the familiar outline of the Eiffel Tower. As always, it stops the heart for just a moment, the lights brightening the darkness, such a symbol of romance and love.
It's a hot night—steamy and awash with the scents of this city. Tourists and perfumeries. Car exhaust and fine wine and freshly baked bread. And life. So much life.
I thought that you should see it."

She sighed softly, closing her eyes for a moment to envision every last detail. Then she opened them again and read the rest of the letter.

As she did so, Annie found herself discovering the City of Lights through the vivid words of a man intimately familiar with it. She also discovered more. With growing certainty, Annie began to understand what Sean was really trying to say.

He was acknowledging the possibilities. Keeping open the chance of a future between them.

Though not overt, his words were letting her know that he was out there, considering…still trying to find a way to let his past and his future come together, and somehow include her.

And he was doing it by giving her the gift he knew she dearly wanted—a glimpse of the big, wide world.

Over the next few weeks, the letters continued. They were sporadic—sometimes several days apart, sometimes two or three in a row. The postmarks varied. He was obviously working—traveling around, being the globe-trotter she knew him to be. And yet he still maintained that connection.

He painted pictures with his words. Amusing her with his descriptions of the driving conditions in Malaysia. Thrilling her as he shared his first impression of the Taj Mahal, the world's great monument to eternal love.

Then one day he wrote from London, describing yet another view from his own bedroom window. Without him saying it, she knew his business was done for a while. He'd gone back to one of those cold, lonely places he called home.

Funny, her own home, which had seemed so empty since he'd left, had begun to feel warm again. Alive. If only because of the way Annie kept reading and rereading the letters, knowing that each one meant she was still on his mind, hopefully, in his heart. Each was worth waiting for, as she'd promised him she would.

Finally, the waiting ended. Because about six weeks after that awful afternoon in his hotel, she opened an envelope to find no letter. Just a plane ticket. And a note.

"Please come see this view for yourself."

Annie didn't even glance at the destination. She was going.

THERE WERE SEVERAL oceans in the world, and Annie had seen none of them.

Sean would someday like to show her the Pacific—to take her to San Francisco so his mother could meet the woman he'd realized he couldn't live without. Then drive down the Pacific Coast Highway, stopping at little wineries and inns. They'd ride with the top down, as they'd done that weekend in June, with the sparkle of waves always visible around the next turn.

He also wanted her to see the other side of that ocean. He'd never been to the South Pacific and could imagine almost nothing better than lying with Annie on the hot, sandy beach of an exotic island, trying to decide whether the water could possibly be as blue as her eyes.

For now, however, not knowing if she had a passport, Sean had decided on the Atlantic.

His choice wasn't merely because of its expediency—since it was closest to Chicago. But also because this was the ocean that touched his homeland, too. Now that he hoped to share his life with Annie, he meant to share *all* of it. Including that troubled part of his past that had yet to be resolved.

He sensed that with her by his side, he could make peace with that past.

"*If* she comes," he reminded himself as he stared out at the water. It glistened now, vivid streams of orange and red—reflections from the sun dropping into the horizon behind him—dancing on the surf.

She'll come.

Sean had never spent much time in Cape Cod, but he'd chosen this place because it reminded him, at least a little, of home. The shoreline wasn't as jagged or rocky, the water and the climate both much warmer. But something about the gray-greenness of the sea and the almost bruised quality of the darkening sky overhead, made him think of Ireland.

Someday he'd go back there. Now that he had someone he wanted to show it to.

Realizing how quickly that sky was darkening, he glanced at his watch. He'd been standing here at the top of a beach crossover for a long time. Annie's flight had been scheduled to land in Boston a few hours ago, and the car he'd had waiting for her at the airport should have had her here by now. *If* she'd been on the plane.

He hadn't even turned his cell phone on, not wanting to get a call from the driver saying she hadn't come. He'd preferred to wait, to stick it out, relying on his certainty that she'd show up, that she wanted this as much as he did.

That she'd understood his letters.

Lost in the rhythmic surge of the surf and the whiteness of the nearly deserted beach, Sean began thinking of the words he would use to describe the precise moment when the light disappeared. In case she didn't see it for herself. In case she wasn't ready and he was forced to keep waiting…keep writing.

In case he'd been wrong.

God, how he hoped he hadn't been wrong.

Fully intent on what he'd do to get her back, he was caught completely by surprise when a voice intruded from behind him.

"It's more beautiful than I ever imagined."

Sean closed his eyes as Annie's soft words washed over him, more welcome and delightful and lovely than the salty breeze skimming across the shoreline.

"Yes, it is," he replied, so relieved he couldn't even turn around.

He remained still and silent. There was so much to say and he'd thought many times of how he'd say it. He needed to tell her where he'd gone, what he'd learned—about himself, about his past, his future. Words to let her know how much he appreciated her faith in him, how glad he was that she had come. Explanations to give about why he'd done what he'd done.

And yet, now, with her warm body moving in close, her soft arms wrapping around his waist from behind, her cheek resting against his back, he wondered if any of them needed to be said at all.

Sean moved his hands to cover hers and they stayed that way, standing motionless on the crossover, for a long time. Until the sun had set, the moon had risen, and the only sound was the never-ending churning of the waves lapping the shore.

And in the shared silence, everything was communicated even though all the words drifted away unsaid.

All but three.

Slowly turning around, Sean looked down at her beautiful face, touching a strand of her moon-kissed hair. And he smiled. Bending toward her, he hesitated for the briefest moment before bringing his lips to hers.

Long enough to whisper those three words. "I love you."

Epilogue

Five Months Later

"ANNIE, SEAN, HURRY up, you're going to be late to your own engagement party!"

Annie, who'd just stepped into her fiancé's arms and lifted hers around his neck so she could draw him down for a kiss, sighed at the sound of her mother's raised voice. She supposed she should be grateful that they'd managed a whole half-hour alone in her old bedroom on the third floor before propriety demanded that *somebody* from her family interrupt.

"I don't suppose there's any escaping?" she asked.

Sean smiled, kissed her on the tip of her nose and murmured, "No, darlin', no escape. You're mine, now."

Liking the way he'd purposely misunderstood her, Annie closed her eyes, savoring his touch.

His mouth moved across to her cheek, then down her jaw. Each brush of his lips on her skin elicited a tiny hitch of a sigh in her throat.

She'd known from the start that Sean was capable of great passion. But, oh, the man's tenderness simply removed the breath from her lungs and filled her with so much lightness she'd swear she could float away.

They'd made love hundreds of times since the night

they'd met, and he could still arouse her with a look. But moments like this truly touched her soul.

"Now, are you ready to be toasted and celebrated by every resident of Green Spring, Illinois?" he whispered before finally pressing his lips to hers for a sweet kiss that removed all worry.

When it ended, though, and he released her, reality quickly returned. "Can't we just skip tonight and proceed right to tomorrow? Christmas Eve is always a lot of fun around here."

He groaned. "Tell me there's no football. I know Jed is looking for some payback for that black eye last summer."

"In the snow? Don't be silly." Teasing him, she lifted a brow. "But, of course, there *is* the polar bear dip."

"I'm afraid to ask."

Though the annual event wouldn't be held until February, she let him worry a little longer. The man was the king of teasing. In the months that they'd been living together in a gorgeous brownstone he'd purchased in Chicago—with a home office he used for his thriving foreign-market consulting business—Sean had proved himself a master at getting exactly the reaction he wanted out of her. In bed, and out.

Especially in.

"The men all get…pissed…on too much beer," she said, having picked up a bit of his lingo in their time together, "and they strip off their clothes and leap into an icy lake."

He visibly shuddered. "I'll pass."

"Chicken?"

He grabbed her and drew her close, cupping her hips, holding her against the full length of his body.

"No, *céadsearc*," he murmured, "just thinking of you and your family."

"Sure," she said softly, not really caring about tormenting him anymore, not when his lips were brushing the edge of her ear and his freshly shaven jaw touching her cheek.

"I wouldn't want your father and brothers seein' me like that."

Shaking off the dazed lethargy that had been washing over her, she tugged away and looked up at him. Grinning, she asked, "Seeing you naked? Why, are you afraid of *shrinkage?*"

Not that he had *any* reason to be. Uh-uh. No way.

She should have known better, should have been warned by the devilish look in his incredible eyes that he'd been setting her up. Because Sean slowly shook his head, visibly trying to look mournful and entirely serious, even though she saw laughter lurking at the corners of his mouth.

"Oh, no. Afraid they'd see how *much* I had and be so worried for your physical comfort, they'd try to prevent you from marrying me."

It took a second for his meaning to sink in, and when it did, Annie threw her head back and laughed. Even as she called him an ass, Sean drew her into his arms again and kissed the laughter from her mouth.

"Come on, you two!" Her mother called out again.

Her spirits much lighter, Annie let Sean lead her out of her old bedroom. How he managed to do it—to arouse her and overwhelm her with tenderness, then tease her into such a good mood, she had no idea. She only hoped he never stopped.

Never.

In the months since that day by the ocean, when he'd

finally let her love him, Sean had done everything in his power to show her he loved her in return. While from very different worlds, they'd managed to create a new one that worked for both of them.

Annie had promoted her assistant manager to handle the day-to-day business at Baby Daze. And Sean had given up his places in London and Manhattan, making Chicago his official "home."

Well, he'd told her that wherever she was would be his official home. Which was just fine with her.

The Paris place he'd kept. Annie had completely fallen in love with the city, and they planned to kick off their round-the-world honeymoon from there.

"Is the entire town going to be here?"

"Of course," she told him as they descended the stairs to the first floor.

The party was set to begin at seven, but even now, at six-thirty, the neighbors had started to arrive. They all greeted Annie with exuberant kisses and hugs, Sean with handshakes and more hugs. Aunts and uncles came loaded with both engagement presents and Christmas ones, neighbors with food and bottles to keep everyone's spirits going strong.

And despite her wish to get on to the holidays—her first with the man she loved—and not make such a big deal out of the engagement, Annie found herself having a wonderful time.

Because she'd also managed to appreciate *this* world, too.

The place she'd been so desperate to escape was, she now acknowledged, part of her. Knowing she never wanted to live out her life in it did not mean she couldn't appreciate the moments she spent here. What could be better than being surrounded by people she loved, who'd do anything to see her happy…even let her go?

Maybe that's why she'd known what to do when she'd reached the moment of truth with Sean. *Let him go.* Because her family had shown her that's what you had to do if you truly loved someone.

It's also what Sean had tried to do for her. He'd wanted to let her go, to *make* her go, so she could escape what he'd believed was his sordid past.

As if she could love him any less for being someone else long ago, when he was the man who filled her heart with joy *now.*

"I love you," she whispered from the corner of her mouth while they posed for another picture. She tried to keep her smile steady—they were waiting for her Great Aunt Trudy's flash to charge back up. A common occurrence tonight.

He made no such effort, turning her to face him, not giving a damn about the camera. "I love you, too." That was when the flash went off.

She'd have to ask for a copy of the picture, wondering if the love she saw shining from every inch of the man's face—and reflecting from hers—could possibly be captured on film.

Throughout the party, Sean remained close by, as if not wanting to leave her side. Even when he was drawn into conversation by one of her brothers or uncles, she always felt his presence. In the middle of the melee, she'd feel the brush of his hand across the back of her neck, or see that smile from several feet away. And they'd silently exchange words, promises, secrets. Almost like the vows they'd be saying out loud just after Valentine's Day.

It was when they were exchanging one of those

warm, hungry gazes that could probably be read by everyone around them that Annie noticed Sean's eyes widening in utter surprise. His mouth pulled into a delighted grin. He walked away from her brother Jed, midsentence, and strode across the room toward the foyer, where her mother had just let in another guest.

When Annie saw the black hair and sweet, laughing face, she knew who the late arrival was.

"Moira," she murmured as she watched her fiancé grab his sister and lift her into a bear hug.

She was so happy for Sean that his sister had made the trip, she wanted to cry. Honestly, she hadn't expected her to, especially this close to Christmas, but there was no way she'd ever have left Moira's name off the guest list. She'd gotten to meet the young woman during a trip to London Annie and Sean had taken last fall, and completely understood why he adored her.

Moira's wasn't the only name on the invitation list that Sean didn't know about. Annie, however, hadn't begun to believe in miracles just because she was now madly in love. So she didn't expect anything to come of *that* invite. She and Sean had talked many times about his issues with his father, and she completely understood—and supported—his need to handle that relationship his own way, whenever he was ready.

But one little invitation—and a few jotted lines of welcome—hadn't seemed too out of line. It had been a tiny hand of peace extended across the ocean, one she had never imagined would be accepted.

Only, she suddenly realized when she saw Sean's face go pale as an older couple followed Moira in, it apparently *had* been.

"Oh, my God," she whispered, watching from

several feet away as Sean stared in shock at the extremely well-dressed couple.

The man's profile was immediately recognizable. Though his hair was more gray than black, his profile hawkish, he had the same bold chin, strong nose, deeply set eyes as his son. This had to be Sean Murphy, Sr.

Forgive me. Part of her was horrified at what she'd done—putting Sean in the position of seeing his father, without warning, for the first time in more than seven years. Another part of her was overjoyed that the older man had unbent enough to come, to take the olive branch she'd extended and return it with his own first step at mending the rift.

At least, she *hoped* that was why he was here. From what Sean told her about the man, his father could be here to drag him away from the nobody-American-farm-girl he'd been stupid enough to propose to.

Ugh. Maybe Sean wasn't the only one in for an incredibly uncomfortable evening.

The two men stood face-to-face for a moment. Moira and the older woman, apparently the stepmother, stepped back to let them talk. Shaken out of her own worry, Annie remembered her manners and hurried toward them. Reaching for Moira, she greeted her with an enthusiastic hug.

"Can you believe he's here?" the girl whispered as she continued the embrace.

"No, honestly, I can't."

Then Annie let her go, turned toward Moira's mother and shook her hand. The woman was very attractive, looking a little like her daughter, but she didn't have the younger woman's warmth. Still, she was polite, and a genuine smile seemed to light up her expression as she watched the Murphy men still talking quietly a few feet away.

As if she felt the tension, Annie's mother joined them, putting a gentle hand on her daughter's shoulder. She didn't know all the details, but she knew enough about Sean's history to realize this was an important moment. All four women watched while everyone else at the party continued their celebration, oblivious to the tension.

Finally, after what seemed like years, but had probably only been a few minutes, a tiny smile softened Sean's perfect mouth. He hadn't even tugged his lips all the way up when the older man in front of him reached out, put his arms around his shoulders, and drew him close.

That paternal embrace had been seven-and-a-half years in the making. So it lasted a long time.

Annie didn't know what had been said, or who had said it. But she knew Sean's eyes were moist and his smile was genuine by the time his father let him go.

All was well. That was all she really *needed* to know.

"Father," Sean said, walking over to slide a possessive arm around her waist, "meet Annie Davis. My future wife." Dropping his hand to her hip and squeezing her lightly, he added, "The woman who helped me figure out who and what I really am. And what I *can* be."

The older man could have resented her. Considering who Sean really *wanted* to be was an independent businessman in Chicago, working to help American companies wade into international markets, the older Murphy could have seen Annie as an enemy. Because Sean would never return to his old life in Ireland, and he had to have told his father that.

But those blue-violet eyes, so much like Sean's—so much like the ones Annie hoped her own children would someday share—were full of nothing but warmth and gratitude.

"I couldn't be happier to meet you, my dear." Her future father-in-law kissed her cheek and squeezed her hand. "You are a most welcome addition to our family."

Annie squeezed back, then looked up at the man she loved, almost unable to believe the way her life had changed in the past several months. Both their lives.

As always, Sean knew what she was thinking. He drew her away to a quiet corner of the room, touching her chin and lifting her face. "Thank you for paying out all that money to give me the happiest Christmas of my life, darlin'."

Confused, she tilted her head. "But I haven't given you your present yet."

"Oh, yes, indeed, you have." He dropped his hands to wrap his arms around her waist and drew her closer. "Last June you paid out five thousand dollars." He kissed her softly, sweetly, with absolute tenderness. "And gave me a whole new reason for existing."

Tears pricking her eyes as she heard the emotion in his voice, Annie could only kiss him back, then repeat what he'd said, knowing he'd given her exactly the same thing.

"A whole new reason for existing. And a *lifetime* to be thankful for it."

Silhouette®
SPECIAL EDITION™

NEW YORK TIMES
BESTSELLING AUTHOR

DIANA PALMER

A brand-new Long, Tall Texans novel

HEART OF STONE

Feeling unwanted and unloved, Keely returns to Jacobsville and to Boone Sinclair, a rancher troubled by his own past. Boone has always seemed reserved, but now Keely discovers a sensuality with him that quickly turns to love. Can they each see past their own scars to let love in?

Available September 2008
wherever you buy books.

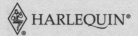

HARLEQUIN®

American ★ Romance®

MARIN THOMAS
A Coal Miner's Wife

HEARTS OF APPALACHIA

High-school dropout and recently widowed
Annie McKee has twin boys to raise. The
now single mom is torn between choosing
charity from her Appalachian clan or leaving
Heather's Hollow and finding a better future
for her boys. But her handsome neighbor and
deceased husband's best friend is determined
to show the proud widow there's nothing
secondhand about love!

*Available August
wherever books are sold.*

LOVE, HOME & HAPPINESS

www.eHarlequin.com   HAR75228

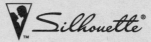

Romantic
SUSPENSE

Sparked by Danger,
Fueled by Passion.

Cindy Dees
Killer Affair

SEDUCTION
SUMMER

Seduction in the sand…and a killer on the beach.

Can-do girl Madeline Crummby is off to a remote
Fijian island to review an exclusive resort, and she hires
Tom Laruso, a burned-out bodyguard, to fly her there
in spite of an approaching hurricane. When their plane
crashes, they are trapped on an island with a serial killer
who stalks overaffectionate couples. When their false
attempts to lure out the killer turn all too real, Tom and
Madeline must risk their lives and their hearts….

**Look for the third installment
of this thrilling miniseries,
available August 2008
wherever books are sold.**

Visit Silhouette Books at www.eHarlequin.com   SRS27594

REQUEST YOUR FREE BOOKS!

2 FREE NOVELS
PLUS 2
FREE GIFTS!

HARLEQUIN®

Blaze™

Red-hot reads!

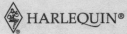

COMING NEXT MONTH

#411 SECRET SEDUCTION Lori Wilde
Perfect Anatomy, Bk. 2

Security specialist Tanner Doyle is an undercover bodyguard protecting surgeon Vanessa Rodriguez at the posh Confidential Rejuvenations clinic. Luckily, keeping the good doctor close to his side won't be a problem—the sizzling sexual chemistry between them is like a fever neither can escape....

#412 THE HELL-RAISER Rhonda Nelson
Men Out of Uniform, Bk. 5

After months of wrangling with her greedy stepmother over her inheritance, the last thing Sarah Jane Walker needs is P.I. Mick Chivers reporting on her every move. Although with sexy Mick around, she's tempted to give him something worth watching....

#413 LIE WITH ME Cara Summers
Lust in Translation

Philly Angelis has been in love with Roman Oliver forever, but he's always treated her like a kid. But not for long... Philly's embarking on a trip to Greece—to find her inner Aphrodite! And heaven help Roman when he catches up with her....

#414 PLEASURE TO THE MAX! Cami Dalton

Cassie Parker gave up believing in fairy tales years ago. So when her aunt sends her a gift—a lover's box, reputed to be able to make fantasies come true—Cassie's not impressed...until a sexy stranger shows up and seduces her on the spot. Now she's starring in an X-rated fairy tale of her very own.

#415 WHISPERS IN THE DARK Kira Sinclair

Radio talk show host Christopher Faulkner, aka Dr. Desire, has been helping people with their sexual hang-ups for years. But when he gets an over-the-air call from vulnerable Karyn Mitchell, he suspects he'll soon be the one in over his head....

#416 FLASHBACK Jill Shalvis
American Heroes: The Firefighters, Bk. 2

Firefighter Aidan Donnelly has always battled flames with trademark icy calm. That is, until a blazing old flame returns—in the shape of sizzling soap star Mackenzie Stafford! Aidan wants to pour water over the unquenchable heat between them. But that just creates more steam....

www.eHarlequin.com

HBCNM0708